THE CASE OF THE
ADVERTISED
MURDER

THE CASE OF THE
ADVERTISED
MURDER

MINNA BARDON

COACHWHIP PUBLICATIONS
Greenville, Ohio

The Case of the Advertised Murder, by Minna Bardon
© 2023 Coachwhip Publications edition

First published 1939
Minna Bardon, 1900-1974
CoachwhipBooks.com

ISBN 1-61646-562-X
ISBN-13 978-1-61646-562-9

ONE

We find plenty of things in advertising departments. That time we used the honeymoon couple in the display windows, and found their own clothes and their shabby suitcase in the outer office, while they had vamoosed with the Chanel suit and the men's tweeds from the "What the Bridegroom Will Wear" display.

But the time Mary Smith came into the advertising department and bunkoed us into letting her stay was still worse. She was a down-at-heels little thing. About twenty-five or thirty, and she fainted clean away when she came to the door of the advertising department. By the time we had her on the couch that they were photographing for the September Sales, she had come to and was looking around sort of frightened. We all rushed to do things for her. Even Charlie, the office boy, ran around with glasses of water in his hand, splashing drops all over the newly typed copy sheets I had just written.

I wanted to take her home with me, or at least get a room for her somewhere, but Mr. Gaines thought it was better not to try to move her at all. He was all for sending for doctors and nurses and setting up a hospital room right there in a corner of the advertising department. I could see right then that Mary Smith was the kind of girl that men do things for.

Finally she started to talk. After we found out that she was hungry and got her fed it was almost in time for the store to close, and we got around to drawing lots over who should take care of her, just as we might have if a stray kitten had been dumped on our doorstep. It never occurred to any of us that Mary Smith was perfectly capable of taking care of herself if we gave her enough for a bed and a few meals.

I remembered afterwards a strange look that passed between her and Mr. Gaines. A sort of see-you-later look. As if they had known each other before and had met by appointment.

Anyhow, Mary Smith went out with Rebecca Allen, leaning a little heavily on Rebecca's angular arm, while Rebecca's sharp face struggled between distaste for the questions that the rest of the bunch was asking Mary, and proud maternal glances at Mary's fragile figure.

We didn't see Mary for three days after that. Rebecca came to her desk the next morning, saying sharply, "Well, are we suckers or aren't we? When I woke up she was gone, with my best nightgown and my new dress. She's probably got some other things, but I haven't had time to look. If she's got my diary and tries to blackmail me I'll kill her."

Most of us felt a little silly at being taken in by a crook just because she was little and helpless and pretty. But advertising people keep on being suckers for the optimism stuff, so we forgot about her soon, except for a few muttered words from Rebecca after she made a trip to her apartment at lunch-time just to see whether Mary had taken her diary.

Mary had. We wondered a little what anybody would want with an old maid's diary, but we laughed. After all, we have a certain respect for Rebecca, who can beat any of us on advertising campaigns and who knows more about merchandise than the merchandise manager.

The next morning I saw Charlie, the office boy, beck-oning me from the corner of the photographer's studio and I thought he probably wanted me to lend him enough change for lunch. Charlie usually runs out of money the day before pay-day and department store lunch-rooms aren't strong on credit.

"Look, Miss Nita," he said. "Take a look at the downy. Somebody's been sleeping on this couch and it wasn't a brunette."

He pointed to the display couch that hadn't been taken back to the furniture department yet, although the photo-grapher had made his pictures.

There was a long, silky thread of hair. It showed up gold against the green rep of the couch-cover.

I remembered back to when Mary Smith had been lying on the couch in her faint. Probably she had lost a stray hair. I said so. But Charlie shook his head.

"This ain't the couch-cover they had on here then," he said. "It didn't look right in the picture and they sent me down to the furniture stock-room for a darker green cover. This was new yesterday. Somebody with yellow hair has been lying on that couch since yesterday. Look there. You can see the marks of a head. And there ain't no blondes in the advertising department."

Faintly, I felt uneasy then. Not for any definite reason. But things began to look a little queer. And the queerness seemed to be attached to a girl who had called herself Mary Smith, who had no money and no place to go and was hungry.

"Maybe one of the buyers came up to bring an ad and lay down to rest," I offered hopefully. Buyers didn't, usu-ally. They were too busy trying to browbeat the advertis-ing department into saying what they wanted them to say about rayon bloomers or aluminum pots and pans. But two of the buyers were blondes, and surely anybody who's tired has a right to take a minute or two off for rest if a couch happens to be handy.

A few minutes later Charlie found the office mouse nibbling at a discarded sandwich crust. After that we found the milk bottles with the remains of coffee in it. And the coffee was still mildly warm.

Prickly feelings began to bother me and I stopped outside Mr. Gaines' office and looked in. He was staring straight ahead of him, without paying any attention to some papers that were on his desk. I cleared my throat and said foolishly, in a way that copywriters sometimes have with good-looking young advertising managers of department stores, "What crime are you plotting?"

He jumped and jerked open a drawer of his desk, thrust the papers in and slammed the drawer. All in a sort of breathless way, while I cleared my throat again and wondered whether he could be writing love letters to Marcia Ames or getting them from her. He grinned in a sickly way and said:

"What did you say, Nita? What do you mean—crime?"

His voice sounded kind of anxious, so I fumbled around and finally blurted out something about how somebody had probably stayed over-night in the store, right here in the advertising department.

"Impossible!" he said sternly. Too sternly, I thought.

After all, it wasn't anything to get so excited about. Nothing important was ever left out overnight here. They had a safe just outside the department to leave valuable things in, and if anybody cared enough for my five-year-old portable typewriter or the artist's drawing board to carry them off, we couldn't do much about it.

Nobody else said anything about the intruder that day. The buyers were coming with the dope for the September Sales and we were trying to calm down the corset buyer who had delusions of grandeur about women's figures and how important her ad should be, and the shoe buyer who wanted to feature evening shoes when we thought he ought to feature shoes to go with Fall suits.

I remember once when I looked for my long, sharp layout shears and accused Charlie of carrying them off to the cut-room the way he did sometimes. He denied having seen them, and we had a little squabble about it until I borrowed the artist's scissors and then it was all right.

Next morning when I saw those shears of mine, they were crusted with something red-brown and sticky, and I could never have used them again for cutting anything even if the police had given them back to me. Which they didn't, of course.

But that was after we found Mary Smith.

Charlie found her. At least we thought then that he was the first to see her.

We all went up that morning in a little rush. We were in the store elevator on its first trip up to the seventh floor. We didn't ride in the employees' elevator because it meant walking halfway down one long corridor and up another. So we just ignored the no-employees-in-elevator rule. And Miss Emily ignored it, too.

Advertising people are supposed to be crazy, after all, and nobody pays much attention to what they do, except when the ads don't pull.

Besides, we were Miss Emily's pets, and Miss Emily was half owner of the store as well as stylist or style merchandiser, or whatever they called her. She had ideas about advertising and they were usually good ideas. I'll say that for her. Except the time she wanted to advertise the murder.

But that comes later. I was walking along the corridor with Marcia Ames, one of the models. She was wearing the Schiaparelli outfit with the fur, and I was trying to tell her that she ought to get a copy of it to be married in. Marcia was engaged to Mr. Gaines, the advertising manager,

which is why she made trips to the advertising department
at every excuse.

She must have gotten to the store very early that day
because she was all dressed, make-up and costume jewelry and everything, by the time I came in and we went up
together.

Her eyes looked sort of bright and glittery, as if she'd
been crying and didn't want anybody to say anything about
it. I noticed that she wasn't wearing her engagement ring
and had on an amethyst instead that matched the purply
glints in her eyes. She kept looking around as if she wanted to see Mr. Gaines and at the same time was terrified at
the idea of seeing him.

Charlie met us at the door with his cap cocked on the
back of his head and a swagger in his walk.

"Hi, Miss Nita," he said, "what would you say to a girl
if she said she liked your hair? You know—just sort of
casually. Could it mean anything? I mean, could you get
anywhere with a girl who was always passing compliments
to all the fellows?" Charlie was always having difficulties
with his current girl-friend and everybody in the store
heard about it and gave him the advice he asked for.

I was laughing and Charlie looked back at me over his
shoulder as he put his hand to the knob of the door to the
advertising office. He turned the knob and nothing happened.

"Look," he said. "Who locked this? It was open last
night. And I was the last one here."

He pounded on the door panel and Marcia and I looked
at each other, a little puzzled. "Maybe Fritz is here," suggested Marcia, blushing a little. Fritz is Mr. Gaines. Nobody else calls him that. But Marcia adores her Fritz and
tells us all about her love affair.

Sometimes we have trouble connecting Marcia's tales of
the love-mad Fritz with dignified, handsome Mr. Gaines,

the advertising manager, but when a man's in love, he's different. And Gaines had been engaged to Marcia for months.

"No, he's not up here," I told Marcia. "Don't you remember? We saw him at the door talking to Lane." Lane's the store detective. One of these fat, good-natured men who was never known to say a harsh word to anybody and who usually found alibis for shop-lifters whether they needed them or not.

"I didn't see him," said Marcia, and when I looked at her suddenly because I thought her voice sounded queer, I thought she looked white under her rouge.

She was looking at the door as you look at the curtain in a theater just before it goes up on a scene that you know will be horrible.

Afterwards I remembered the look. But then I just thought she had quarreled with her Fritz and had probably come to make up.

Charlie pounded on the door a little and then he said, "I'll get in through the cut-room. This is one of those locks that open from the inside without a key. Half a minute."

We saw him swaggering down the corridor and disappear into the cut-room and then, five minutes later, he came out again, looking a little green. He said:

"Get Lane, somebody. And the cops. She's been murdered. Her throat's cut!"

I shuddered a little just from looking at him before I could really take in his words. They didn't seem to mean anything. He said impatiently:

"Ain't anybody going? I got to stay here myself and see that nobody spoils any clues or anything."

He was still green, but sounded a little cross. As if he were impatient because somebody was trying to stop him from doing what he wanted to do.

I said stupidly: "You're joking, Charlie." And I laughed a little, I think. Silly things you do.

"Shut up, Nita," he said. I think I was more surprised that he called me Nita without the Miss than that he told me to shut up. It sounded as if he had suddenly grown up all at once, in spite of the cocky cap and the schoolboy suit.

It was real, then. Murder.

I said it, in a whisper, I think: "Murder." He nodded and Margaret moaned a little. Watching Marcia's face, I asked him, "Not Gaines?"

Charlie shook his head. "That little crook," he said, very quietly. "Mary Smith, she called herself. She's got her throat cut and the whole floor is bloody and she's got on Miss Rebecca Allen's best dress." After a pause he added:

"Don't let anybody go in, and you stay out, too. I'm getting the police. Lane ought to handle this. I'll help him. He's never seen anything like this."

We saw him go sprinting down the corridor with his coat flashing out behind him and his footsteps making a sort of tattoo sound on the floor.

Marcia put her hand out blindly and I took it. Tears were falling on the Schiaparelli model and neither of us cared at all. Marcia said very firmly;

"He didn't do it, Nita. My Fritz didn't kill her. He'd have found some other way of getting rid of her. I know it."

"Of course he didn't," I agreed. Then I saw the misery in her lovely eyes and I went cold inside. Because I felt that somehow Marcia believed Fritz guilty of the murder.

Pretty soon Charlie was back with Lane beside him. They both went in and came out again and stood there with us, in a sort of huddle around the advertising department door.

"I called the police," Lane said, in his husky voice. "They said to keep everybody out."

There was a staccato of sharp-heeled footsteps along the corridor and Miss Emily Paul came up behind us. Every tidy curl on her head was fastened with its invisible hairpin; every fold in her ruffles neatly starched and crisp; her shoes as polished as if she took them off and carried them in her pocket when she walked on dirty streets.

"Quite right," said Miss Emily. "Keep everybody out. I'll take the key until the police come."

She held out her hand and Lane reluctantly gave her the key. She looked at it thoughtfully, then disappeared down the corridor in the direction of the cut-room, with Lane blundering after her. I could hear the protesting tones of his voice without being able to understand the words. But Miss Emily went straight on, shaking her head at him. She turned the key in the lock, opened the door and went in.

TWO

Miss Emily Paul didn't come out of the same door through which she went in. Instead, we heard the knob to the outer ad office door turn and Miss Emily's face appeared, looking just as neat and self-possessed as if a multiplication table were hidden in the office instead of a dead body.

She didn't even look pale. I heard Marcia gasp a little and neither Marcia nor I stepped forward when she said "Come in," as if she were a hostess welcoming us to a tea-table.

Lane said: "Now look here, Miss Emily. The police ain't going to stand any monkeying with clues or anything. That's my job, to keep people out. After all," he added, defensively, "I am the store detective." As if he were reminding himself of it. I felt a little like that, too. I didn't feel like Nita Manners, copywriter in the advertising department of E. & B. Paul Department Store.

I didn't feel like much of anything just then. But Miss Emily stepped aside and then I felt like a person about to be acutely seasick. Because I saw Mary Smith then.

The gash across the throat, first, looking like a second mouth, grotesquely open and grotesquely brown-red. There was blood on her dress, too. The dress looked much more familiar than the face I had seen once before, and then I remembered that Mary Smith had walked off with

Miss Rebecca Allen's new dress and best nightgown and diary, besides a few other things that Rebecca hadn't mentioned.

I peered around Miss Emily, staring at the body like any gaping sightseer, feeling ashamed of myself for my curiosity and then more nauseated by the sight of the blood and the glittery open eyes. They didn't look horrible, those eyes, but terribly stupid. I kept wishing somebody would close them so that Mary Smith wouldn't watch me eternally from her huddled position on the floor of the ad office.

We've had plenty of excitement in the advertising office before, but nothing like the hour after we discovered Mary Smith's body.

I had always thought of policemen as protective heroes, but the ones who came that day looked a little sleepy as if they'd been up too long. One of them was chewing at the end of a ragged-looking, home-rolled cigarette and searching for stray flakes of tobacco with his tongue.

I couldn't tell the policemen apart at first. They got us all out of the place pretty soon and herded in Mr. Gaines' private office the way we were when we had style conferences. The buyers were all there and the whole advertising department. Miss Emily Paul, too, and her brother, Mr. Bertram Paul, who thought he was running the store because somebody had put "President and General Manager" after his name on the glass door of his office.

He kept looking around him with that shy, ineffectual manner of his until Miss Emily gave him some paper and a pencil and asked him to make a list of something or other.

He was looking intently at the list when the policemen came back in the room and took their places at the door and on the stand where the models usually posed to show us the new merchandise before it was put in stock.

After a while I found out that the tall man with the ragged cigarettes was in charge. He just sat there for a few minutes, looking at some cards he had in his hand, and licking his mouth with the tip of his tongue to find a stray fleck of tobacco. I couldn't stand it any longer, so I took out my cigarette case and handed it to him. He looked blank for a minute, then grinned a kind of a nice grin and took a cigarette. He played with the case for a minute or two. Then he grinned again and stuck it in his pocket, and if he didn't wink at me he almost did.

It kind of got me back to normal again so that I got control of myself. After all, it was pretty bad, but it could have been worse. Mary Smith wasn't anything to us. Just a poor stray cat that we'd picked up and that had scratched us. Miss Rebecca, anyhow. Because if you give food and shelter to a person you don't expect to have her steal your clothes.

The policeman was talking. His voice sounded nice, too. Kind of strong and reliable. Steady. You could depend on him. He said:

"Sorry to keep you all here, but we'd like to get to the bottom of this business right away. This girl got hers here, and without too much yapping we've got to get the guy that did her in."

"Guy—or gal," put in a matter-of-fact voice from a runty little man next to him. "By the time you've done all the leg work and get to using your head, you'll find it's a gal. The old jealousy racket. You can count on it, Hank."

Hank took another puff on my cigarette and didn't say anything. He just put something down on one of his cards with a pencil he had swiped from the ad office some where. We all use those bright blue drawing pencils for writing rough copy. People are always carrying them off.

Lane came in about that time, looking plenty troubled. He said: "Hank, how about letting me ask questions? I know all these people. I can ask 'em questions without hurting their feelings."

Hank was the man with my cigarettes, of course. He seemed to be somebody important. I learned afterwards that he was a detective inspector who had done a lot of leg work and regular police routine before he got to where he was now—wherever that was. But in the meantime he was just somebody we watched and who watched us, and you could feel a sort of wall of fear and anxiety between him and the rest of us that belonged in the store.

"Look here, Lane," Hank said, after a final puff on his cigarette, "these people are in the deep in this. The girl out there in that office is dead, and somebody killed her. Dollars to doughnuts it's somebody in this room, and if it wasn't they've got to show me. If anybody's going to worry about hurting their feelings it's not me."

He threw his head up, straightened his shoulders and punched out the stub of his cigarette in a way that I liked. As if he'd get to the bottom of this business or know the reason why. I think maybe I really started liking him then. Liking him a lot.

Maybe he had a wife in Baltimore and one in Reno, but I kind of liked the sound of his voice and the way he looked and talked.

I wondered whether a detective inspector made enough to get married on. But that was a little premature. We were starting to talk about the murder. Really talk.

We all answered a lot of questions and then Hank took Mr. Gaines into the little cut-room to answer some questions privately. One policeman had a notebook and made shorthand hieroglyphics. When the rest of us finished talking, the policeman followed Gaines and Hank into the cut-room and we were left in the care of a third officer.

Nobody said anything for a little while. Then Miss Emily said abruptly: "The September Sales."

Startled, I raised my eyebrows at her. She nodded. "It'll give them something," she announced. "Nobody's ever had any publicity like this before. Everybody'll want to see the place where it happened and we'll make money on it."

Marcia moaned a little. "Don't, Miss Emily! How can you? This is murder, not just a publicity stunt."

Miss Emily silenced Marcia with a stern glance. "Girl," she said, "what are you doing here? This was supposed to be a meeting of executives and buyers and the advertising department. You're a dress model."

"I know," admitted Marcia meekly. "But I'm engaged to the advertising manager. That's why they told me to be here."

"Engaged! Nonsense. Nobody's engaged to Mr. Gaines," said Miss Emily firmly. "I have reason to know." And she firmly closed her thin lips and looked Marcia up and down in that searching way she has.

Hank came back about that time, with Mr. Gaines looking rather green and flabby. Mr. Gaines gave Marcia a sickly smile and sat down in a corner with his head leaning on his hand. Marcia started up from her seat as if she were about to go to him, but Hank beckoned her and she reluctantly followed him into the cut-room.

Lane said: "Miss Emily, I want to help, but they won't let me." He sounded a little helpless.

"Mind your own business, Lane," she said. "This is their affair. All it means to us is a little inconvenience for a few days and the loss of a day's sales which we'll more than make up in the September Sales, if we handle this publicity right. That's what we've got to think of now. Of course they've closed the store for today. Rather, they didn't really let it open. There were only a couple of customers in when they found the body, and they're herded in the big hall with the employees, telling policemen that they don't know anything at all about it."

She was as cool as an iced cucumber salad. Yet I rather welcomed her poise, because it kept the rest of us from getting hysterical. After all, this business wasn't any affair of ours and although I thought Miss Emily was wrong about advertising the murder—still, it was something to be considered. I welcomed anything that meant work to keep my mind off the horror of that figure on the floor of the outer ad office.

Miss Emily called: "Gaines, come here!"

As feebly as if he had been ill for a long, long time, Mr. Gaines arose from his chair and came over to where we were sitting. He slumped down into a chair near us, and Miss Emily started on him.

"Get out your copy-paper, Gaines." You'd have thought that he was an office boy or the newest cub copywriter, but he thrust a hand aimlessly into his pockets and brought it out with some paper in it. The yellow paper we used for copy sheets in the department. It wasn't until later that I saw the blotch of blood on the paper. Not until after he had filled a couple of pages with scrawls that Miss Emily dictated, and had turned another page for a fresh sheet.

"The headlines first. Let's get a good list of them," proclaimed Miss Emily firmly.

She consulted with herself for a minute. Her eyes were tightly closed behind her glasses and her lips moved in tempo with her thoughts.

"The first headline is easy," she said, *"Even Murder Couldn't Stop This Sale!"*

Obediently Gaines' pencil moved over the yellow paper as if guided automatically by Miss Emily's thoughts.

I said: "They won't let you print it that way, Miss Emily. The newspapers or the police department will stop the ad."

"Then I'll take my advertising away from the papers and advertise by direct mail," she said. "If that won't bring them to time, nothing will. They'd print the account of a murder before it happened for an advertising appropriation the size of mine, and don't you let them tell you anything different."

One by one the buyers were awakening to the plans that were going on and they began to brighten up. Mr. Willing, the shoe buyer, straightened up and took out a handkerchief to mop his bald head. Miss Tates, the corset buyer, patted the crisp ruffles on her broad bosom and gave the little wriggle that meant she was settling herself into her corselette. Miss Emily was talking business and the buyers were ready for action. Miss Tates said eagerly:

"There's a little number I thought we ought to feature if we have space enough. It's an extra-size garment with the lines of uplift."

"Burlesque stuff," sniffed Mrs. Plaut, the coat buyer. "Nobody has a figure like that any more. You're kidding yourself."

"Just because you look like a string-bean yourself," accused Miss Tates, "you think nobody has a right to a womanly figure. Now the figure that men really prefer—"

A titter came from Mr. Willing's prim mouth. "The figure men prefer," he said, "is any figure they can get to put their arms around. I heard that at the Empress last week. Pretty good, eh, Tates?" He gave her a rakish poke somewhere within the bounds of her own well-corseted figure and she smiled a little uncertainly.

"Nonsense," Miss Emily broke in. "We won't have to bother about goods, or prices. Boost up all the prices a cent or two and make it pay for the business we're losing today. You, Willing, put out those high oxfords for fall suits at $7.95 instead of $7.50. They're good values at that, and what's the use of such a small margin of profit if we can get the people in the store anyhow?"

"But, Miss Emily," protested Willing uneasily, "Walter Edmunds is selling that same number for $7.30."

"Fine," Miss Emily said. "Put two pairs of the shoes on stands next to each other. Put signs on both of them. On one say: 'This is our own model, the best that can be made.' On the other, say: 'This is a copy of our shoe that was made to be sold cheaply by other stores. It looks the same, but a few weeks' wear will tell the difference.'"

Knowing Miss Emily and her methods, I still gasped a little. She was full of ideas like that. It was a shame that her talents should be wasted on a small department store in a mid-west town. She'd have made a fortune in lumber or railroads a generation ago. Shrewdness like that might not be straight, but it was profitable. For Miss Emily and her brother Bertram, who were co-owners of the store.

She went on that way, showing her familiarity with every item scheduled for promotion in the September Sales, including even the couch on which we had put Mary Smith on her first visit to the store.

Hearing them talk about the couch brought me back to the day before when Charlie had shown me Mary Smith's golden hair on the couch-cover. I hadn't a doubt that she had found her way into the store and had slept on the couch. She had obviously brought in with her some coffee in a milk bottle, and a sandwich. Yet if she had brought them in with her and had spent the night there, why hadn't the coffee in the bottle been cold when we found it? And why hadn't the crust that Charlie scared the mouse away from been stale?

Mr. Gaines, by this time, had filled two pages of the paper with the stuff that Miss Emily dictated about the ad changes, and it was when he turned to the third page that I saw the blotch of red-brown right in the middle of the sheet, with the yellow of the paper puckered around it. Mr. Gaines looked stupidly at the blood spot and then, in a tired way, just closed his eyes and slumped down in his chair.

It was just at that minute that Marcia came out of the cut-room followed by Hank. When she saw Gaines she ran to him and, cradled his head in her arms and began to croon, "Fritz—oh, my Fritz," like a mother singing a baby to sleep.

THREE

I didn't want to go away and leave them because I felt that something was going to happen. But Hank beckoned to me and, with a reluctant look over my shoulder, I followed him into the cut-room.

Hank closed the door after me and waved me to a seat on one corner of the table where we kept the bound newspapers. With the help of an astonishingly strong hand I got myself up on top of a bound volume and the policeman took his place near the door on a box that somebody had pulled in from the shipping-room. Hank was standing, towering above me.

Maybe I was just nervous when I said to him, "Sit down, why don't you? You look so big I'm scared."

"That's why I'm big, to scare you into making a confession or something," he said. But he grinned, and perched himself on another corner of the table.

"Now that we're alone," I began, and then, unaccountably, found myself feeling red in the face. Funny what a policeman can do to you.

Businesslike, he asked: "Tell me all you know about this girl, won't you, Miss Nita? They told me your name, you see. By the way, I don't suppose you did it, but it's customary to warn you that anything you say can be taken down and used against you. So if you did it, you'd better shut up until you find a mouthpiece."

There I was in the cut-room of the advertising department where I earned my living, talking to a detective inspector and feeling friendlier toward him than I'd felt toward any man in a long time.

"I didn't kill Mary Smith," I said. "But she was a prize-winning rat, from what I know of her, so she's better off as she is. Couldn't you just call it a day and go home?"

Not that I thought he would, but it sounded like a good idea.

He looked at me and frowned. "When did you know her? What do you know about her? It's great, working in a store like this. Everybody knows everybody else's secrets and nobody's talking."

"Well, it was like this," I began. "The girl came into the advertising department and gracefully fainted on the floor. Right about in the same position that she is now." I stopped and felt a little jittery, remembering.

"Go on."

"Well, we picked her up, put her on the couch, and fussed around her. She said she was Mary Smith and she was hungry and didn't have any place to go. That's all any of us knows about her, except—"

"Except that somebody killed her?"

"Except that she went home with one of the women in the department who offered her a place to sleep. During the night she walked off with half the things in the woman's apartment."

"I've known girls like that. They'd take your false teeth and your wig."

"Mary took Rebecca Allen's new dress and best nightgown. Also a diary of some kind."

"What did you say?" he asked sharply. "A diary?"

"Um-huh. Funny what women will do with their spare time, isn't it? Miss Rebecca's a nice old maid, but she has secrets. She said if Mary Smith tried to blackmail her with the stuff in the diary she—"

At that point I realized that I was talking to somebody in the police department and shut up. If Miss Rebecca killed her, I wasn't going to put her in danger.

"I see. Rebecca said she'd kill the girl if she blackmailed her. That was it, wasn't it?" He seemed almost indifferent.

I don't know why I nodded. After all, I'd never seen this man before and I considered Miss Rebecca one of my best friends. That's what loyalties between women are, I thought disgustedly. At the first question from a man, they vanish.

"She didn't kill her," I said defensively. "Rebecca couldn't kill anybody. She talks a lot, but it doesn't mean anything."

"The people who do the talking aren't the ones who do the killing, usually," he comforted me. "Besides, we haven't any evidence that she blackmailed Miss Rebecca. When did she say that?"

I counted back. "It was yesterday that we found the hair on the couch. I'll tell you about that in a minute. And it must have been the day before that Miss Rebecca said it."

He thought a minute and watched the stubby fingers of the policeman making notes. "Tell me about the hair on the couch, please."

I told him all about the changed couch-cover and how it was impossible that Mary Smith had left the gold hair on the cover when she had been lying there. I reminded him that it might have been some other blonde. There were plenty of blondes in the store. And then I remembered about the sandwich that wasn't stale and the coffee that wasn't cold.

He was thoughtful. "If she had brought the stuff in with her the day before, the coffee would have been cold and the bread staler. That sounds right, doesn't it?"

"That's what I made it," I agreed. "She could have hidden in the store, I guess—washrooms or some place—and come out after the store was closed, to sleep on the couch. She knew the couch was there because she was put on it when she fainted. But why did she come to the store in the first place? And how did she get the fresh sandwich yesterday morning and the hot coffee at the same time? Unless somebody brought it to her."

"Somebody brought it to her if she didn't get it for herself. She didn't, if there wasn't any way for her to get out at night and get back in again before the store opened without upsetting the burglar alarm system."

"That's okay, Lane would know about it."

"I'll check that with him, then. So she slept on the couch and somebody brought her a sandwich and coffee for breakfast in the morning. She ate it before the store opened and was gone before you got to the department at—nine?"

"Listen, I get there at nine, but the store hour is eight-thirty. Let's call it that just to save my job for me. They'll make me start punching the time clock again any day now," I told him confidentially.

"Let's call it whatever you say. Were you the first one there?"

I thought a minute. "Charlie said he discovered this business at about ten, and he told me later. I can ask him the time. I didn't notice it."

"What I'm trying to get into the heads of all you people," said Hank, "is that this is a murder. M-U-R-D-E-R. Look it up in your dictionary sometime. Maybe you didn't like this woman, but she had a right to live, anyhow. How'd you like to have somebody come up behind you with a pair of sharp scissors and slit your throat?"

I shuddered. "Not very pleasant." Then I thought of what he'd said, and I felt a little woozy. "Did you say scissors?" I asked. "Not a long pair of sharp office shears? Tailoring shears, really, I guess. Blades a foot long and very sharp. Steel handles banded with black. A red ribbon tied on one of the handles."

"That's it," he said quietly. "Yours?"

"Mine. I use them to do layouts with. I'm supposed to be a copywriter, but in a store like this everybody does everything. We use the shears to cut out proofs and all sorts of odds and ends around the office. Mr. Gaines sent them out to be sharpened last week because he tried to cut something with them and said that good, self-respecting butter couldn't be cut with them."

"I see. Did Gaines see this girl?"

I thought there was some catch about that question. After all, he had talked to Gaines first. And he had said something pretty bad to make Gaines come out of the room looking like a damp washrag.

I said, to hide my rising anger: "I won't bite. Ask Gaines."

I didn't meet his eyes. For a minute I hated him. Then it occurred to me that you didn't go around hating men whose names you didn't even know except for the nickname Hank. Silly name—Hank. Looked like him, too. Kind of big and broad and dependable. Not one of those slick policemen always trying to catch you up. And he was that kind, really, in spite of his looks.

He said surprisingly: "Look here. My name's Hank Bemis. Henry Bemis. You're Nita. What's the rest? Manners, isn't it? Now, Nita Manners, let's get this straight. I like you. You know it. You like me. I can tell it. Well, what's going to happen to that? You see, I'm being frank."

"I don't know what you mean," I answered. But I did. He said:

"Oh, I'm not talking about love at first sight or any dope like that. You can see that on the screen. But you're the kind of a girl I like and I'm looking for a girl. Haven't had time for one so far. No policeman pounding a beat should take time for women. Besides, I don't like all women. I like a girl with some sense to her and some looks to her. You mightn't think it to look at me, but—"

A cough from the policeman with the notebook and the broad grin interrupted him. "Look, Clancy," Hank said, his ears red, "you try repeating this in the back-room and I'll tell about the time you made the date with the broad on Atlantic Street. Now look, Clancy, you go and get those notes transcribed. Tell Riley to get Lane to help him question the others. I'm going to be busy here for a few minutes."

"I see," said Clancy and winked at me. I winked back, to my own surprise, and he looked surprisingly approving.

Well, we were alone, then, and I didn't know what to say or do. I wasn't much for men. Most of them seemed to be such weak sisters. But this one had something that got me somehow. And it made me a little flustered to have him talking so straightforward.

"Nita," said Hank, "we'll work this business together. You're the only person in this place I'm sure of. If you tell me you didn't do it, I believe you. But I don't know who to believe of the others. Play along with me, Nita. I need your help."

"Policeman woos maid to get evidence," I said, flippantly, and then he grabbed me. He held my arm so tight that I had a bruise the next day. He said:

"You know better than that, Nita. I could slap you down for that, and if you do it again I will. I'm straight on this. You know it. You're a girl I like and you know it. Whether you help me or not it'll be the same. Even if you keep me from getting a conviction, it'll be the same. Know it, Nita?"

Looking into his eyes, I knew it, and said so. This was different somehow, and it made me feel warm and contented. Because something pleasant was happening to me in spite of all the horrible things that were happening in the store.

He didn't make any effort to kiss me. He just looked at me a little longer, as if he were studying my face and trying to read me a little. He lifted me down from the table and held me tight for a minute before he put me on my feet.

Then he went to the door and went out, closing it behind him and I was alone, looking at the closed door behind which he had disappeared and the other closed door behind which so much was going on. I heard voices and the sound of a camera dragged across the floor. Somebody said: "One more shot of this." And somebody else said: "Where are the guys with the basket?"

I couldn't count how many people were there, but I just stood and stared at the closed door. Finally it opened and I saw a bunch of people, with Hank standing there watching me.

"In again, out again," I said, as gaily as I could. He nodded.

"I went in at the other door," he said. "Come in here, Nita. It'll be bad, but you're big enough to stand it. I want to know whether there's anything more you can tell me."

Reluctantly I walked to the door and hesitated there. When Hank took my hand I stopped hesitating and walked right in. Mary Smith didn't look half so horrible as I had expected. They had drawn a chalk line around her as she lay huddled on the floor. It looked rather like the frame around a picture, and increased the illusion of unreality.

Somebody had turned her a little, so that the wound was not quite so evident. The gash didn't look like a second open mouth any more, and Mary looked sort of frail and pathetic. More like she had looked that other day when she fainted on the floor.

"You recognize her well enough to identify her?" asked Hank gently. His hand was still on my arm.

"Yes. As well as you can identify anybody you've only seen once. But I know her dress. It's the one she stole from Miss Rebecca. She's wearing Miss Rebecca's shoes, too. I know that pair with the blue gabardine bands. Mr. Willing ordered them for Miss Rebecca."

Then my eyes were caught by the girl's slim, colorless hand and I said, before I realized what I was saying: "Why—that's Marcia Ames' engagement ring. So that's why Marcia wasn't wearing it."

Hank gave a sigh of relief and he said: "So that's where it came from. Clancy, tell 'em to wait outside with the basket for a few minutes and get Marcia Ames in here. I want her to identify her ring."

FOUR

When Marcia came in she kept her eyes away from the girl on the floor and came straight to me with hands outstretched. I held them. Hank moved away a little and dropped his hand from my arm and I was conscious of missing his touch. This was pretty bad. I'd have to look after this. To think of any man having that effect on me after a little while. Yesterday I'd never heard of him. I turned to Marcia. Gently I asked her:

"Have you lost your engagement ring, Marcia?" I heard Hank give a little gasp, but he didn't say anything.

Marcia sobbed a little, without closing her eyes, and the tears standing there against the blue were almost too much for me. She nodded. "I've lost the ring, Nita. I'll never see it again. Even if we found it again, now, I wouldn't want it after she's had it on her hand."

Hank asked sharply from behind us: "She? You mean Mary Smith?"

"I mean Mary Gaines. She was Fritz Gaines' wife once. They were divorced. They never really lived together except for a few weeks. Then she came here. We were so happy— and now it's all gone away—all the happiness."

"So that's it," said Hank, as if to himself. "You got it, Clancy?"

Clancy nodded. I turned around and frowned at him and then at Hank. How *could* they?

"How did she get your ring?" asked Hank.

"She said she'd make trouble. She said she'd find a way of invalidating her divorce so that our marriage wouldn't be legal. So there'd be a scandal in the store and Fritz would lose his job."

"Your marriage?" Hank asked gently, prodding her. I hated him.

"We're married. We've been married for months. But my mother's not expected to live and we thought it would be easier if I'd stay with her and keep her happy for her last few weeks. But—we've been together on week-ends. And—it would have been terrible if Mary had done what she said—about her divorce. Because I'm going to have a baby."

"That does it," said Hank with a note of satisfaction that I hated. I turned on him. I even forgot the silent figure on the floor at my feet and the girl whose hand I held. There was nobody in the room, so far as I was concerned, except me and this tall, lanky so-and-so whom I couldn't help liking—and hating.

"You're leading her on to say things she shouldn't," I accused him. "You didn't warn her the way you warned me. You're making her say things she'll hate herself for. You're making her betray the man she loves. How'd you like it if a girl did that to you—*your* girl?"

He came and took my hand. The other hand. I was still holding Marcia's cold fingers. He said: "If Gaines killed her, they'll understand that it was self-defense in its way. I'll promise you that, Nita, And if he didn't kill her, he has nothing to fear from the truth. I like your loyalty, Nita. If you can be that way for a friend, what would you be for a sweetheart?"

He looked so human and so dependable that I sort of calmed down and I turned to Marcia and said: "I guess he understands, kid. If anybody can help you, Hank can."

"But Fritz didn't kill her. Tell him that my Fritz couldn't kill anybody," begged Marcia.

"He's a lucky man to have your love," said Hank gently. "If he didn't kill her I can promise you that we won't hurt him. We only want the truth, Miss Marcia. Help us to find the truth."

"I'll help you," she said, miraculously calm all at once. I saw that she, too, was impressed by Hank's steadiness and sincerity.

He took out a ragged, hand-rolled cigarette, started to light it, then, remembering, tossed it into the wastebasket and took another cigarette out of the case I had given him.

"Your mind must be wandering, Hank," said Clancy. "You threw your cigarette in that wastebasket and they haven't finished with the room yet. Where's your head? You're in love, maybe?"

"Maybe," Hank agreed, bending down to fish the cigarette out of the waste-basket. "Mess in here," he said, looking down into the basket.

"It's not clues," I said hurriedly. "Just a bunch of stuff I cleared out of my desk drawers. They won't put those torn-up letters together and read them, or anything like that, will they, Hank?"

They were silly things. Letters from a man who'd imagined he liked me once. A couple of pressed flowers from a corsage. Foolish things like that. I'd cleaned out my desk, stuffed the crumpled letters and dusty flowers into a big envelope, and sealed the whole business. I'd have hated Hank to see those silly letters. Men write stupid letters sometimes and girls keep them, even if they don't like the men much. Because, after all, it's something to know that somebody feels that way about you. On days when your new shoes hurt or the purple blouse isn't nearly as becoming as you thought it might be.

Hank took out the sealed envelope. "This? Anything else?"

"Nothing." He took the envelope, folded it, and tucked it into an extra-wide pocket in the inside of his coat. "I won't open it if I can help it and I won't let it get out of my hands, Nita. I promise you."

That wasn't much help, because I wasn't anxious for *him* to see the letters. In fact, I think then I'd rather have trusted Clancy with them.

Well, they weren't important, anyhow, but I certainly didn't want them connecting silly letters written to me with a murder case.

Marcia said anxiously to Hank: "You'll save him for me, won't you?"

"If he didn't do her in," promised Hank, "you can have him for keeps and nobody'll try to take him away from you."

I liked him a lot then and I guess I showed it by the look I gave him. Anyhow, he kind of brightened up until his glance fell on the body at our feet.

Funny how callous you get, after a little while. It seemed to me, suddenly, as if the limp, huddled figure didn't have anything of more human quality than the dummies we used in the store windows to display new dresses for sales. There was something of that same waxen look about the features, and the eyes looked just as brightly painted and stupid as those other eyes that stared out over the shopping crowds.

It made me feel a little better to think that way. I even began to feel a little sorry for Mary Smith, so that anger lost its place to sympathy. No matter what cheap little tricks she had done, she didn't deserve this. Even if she had done her best to break up the love that existed between Gaines and Marcia, surely neither one of them could have done anything so—so terribly *final* to her.

I took a step forward to see her better, and Marcia looked too. She gasped a little, but held up bravely when she saw her ring, with its odd setting and its glittering facets, on that hand that looked so artificial.

"She looks so young now, and so sweet," said Marcia surprisingly, "that I can't believe she said the things she said or did the things she did. Oh Nita, you just wouldn't believe the way she talked to me and the way she acted to my poor darling Fritz. She hated him for not loving her. She wanted to break up our marriage just because she couldn't make a success of being married to him. I hated her then, and now I can't hate her, seeing her like this. Fritz didn't do it, Nita—did he?"

She stopped, as if frightened at her own words, and looked around. Hank didn't seem to be listening or watching, but in a minute after she had looked back at Mary, he motioned with his head toward the cut-room door and Marcia and I went on out.

They didn't seem to want us back in the room where the rest of them were, so we went on down the deserted stairs. The elevators weren't running. The operators were probably being questioned somewhere, and so were the stock-girls and sales-people, as well as the executives. The store was deserted, still hooded in its night canvases of dirty white, spread over display tables in the aisles and over shining glass counter-cases.

There were September Sale banners and posters everywhere and a few photographs on bulletin boards, with signs saying: "Ask for these in our 'September Sales.'" All the promotion we'd been working on for months.

This morning we'd planned to get all the ends tied up so that the next morning we'd be ready to start the sale.

Fortunate that all this had happened today and not tomorrow. We strolled up one deserted aisle and down another.
Now and then we came on policemen poking their way
around uncertainly as if searching for clues.

But they didn't seem to know a clue from a September
Sale item, so they just fumbled around and didn't do much
of anything.

Then we came on Miss Tates crying in a corner. Her
black satin dress with its crisp white collar seemed to be
wilting on her, and her face was streaked with her suntan
powder that had developed darker tan splotches.

Marcia went to her with that quick, sympathetic way
she has, and put an arm around her. "Tell me what's the
matter, Miss Tates. Anything new? Have they been doing
things to you, too?"

Miss Tates gulped a time or two and managed to control her voice. "They know that I knew she was here," she
said. "I brought her sandwiches and coffee yesterday."

"Why—why did you, Miss Tates?" Marcia couldn't seem
to understand it.

"Because I had to. She said if I didn't she'd tell something that would make me lose my job. If I'd known what
I know now, I'd have died first."

A policeman came a little nearer and peered at us from
behind a counter, trying to hear what Miss Tates was saying.

Promptly she stopped talking and shut her mouth into
a prime rosebud shape that looked strangely incongruous
on her cheerfully plump face.

Marcia suggested: "Maybe they'd let us go to the lunch-
room and see if there's anybody there to make us some coffee. Or I could make some if nobody's there. Surely there's
coffee in the supply cupboard."

The steps were long and narrow. Nobody ever used
them. They were just there to comply with the fire regu-
lations. We had taken elevators so much for granted that

now when the elevators were quiet little rooms in cages instead of moving walls, we hardly knew how to get up or down in the store.

The steps made us breathless, but finally we got up to the lunch-room and found that everybody else who had finished with the examinations had the same idea. One of the cooks was on duty and a couple of the stock-girls were acting as waitresses. Somebody had made coffee and toast, and they had taken a big cheese and a huge pot of jam from the delicatessen department. Nobody was paying for anything.

"It's all on the house," Charlie said to me, appearing out of a corner where he was sitting with a pretty stock-girl. She was probably the one he had asked my advice about earlier this morning. The girl who "passed compliments to all the boys." Well, she had the right idea, judging from the complacency in Charlie's face as she listened and commented while he told her about his part in the gruesome discoveries of the morning.

Somebody brought us coffee and toast that wasn't especially hot. There wasn't enough butter, but we cut great slabs of cheese and speared them with knives that somebody had left on the tables. We had paper plates for the rather commercial-tasting jam, and evaporated milk for the coffee.

Things began to look a little festive. People were calling from one table to another and it was all very merry. For everybody except that poor soul in the advertising office, who had probably deserved everything she got. But that didn't make it any easier.

I sort of looked around for Hank. Not that he'd be there. He was probably downstairs asking questions. I wondered if he hated to ask them as much as other people hated to answer them. But, after all, he wouldn't be a detective if he hated asking questions.

I took my cup to the counter to have some more coffee put into it.

"Make it two," said a voice behind me, and I jumped so I spilled the coffee all over my new suit.

It was Hank.

He handed back my cup for refilling and while the counter-girl was attending to it and one for him, he mopped at my suit with a frayed white handkerchief. When he took both of our cups of coffee and followed me to the table where Marcia and Miss Tates were waiting, I surprised myself by feeling a little light-headed. Sort of drunk on coffee—or something.

"Well," said Hank, putting both cups on the table, "I've found a murderer."

FIVE

I saw Marcia Ames catch at the edge of the table. Her eyes fluttered and then opened wide. "Not my Fritz," she begged.

Her Fritz. Her husband. I had forgotten they were married. She had been Marcia Ames to me for a long time.

Hank shook his head. "It isn't your Fritz," he said. "It might even be a woman. We've found out a few things."

He looked at Miss Tates and it was her turn to look flustered. I remembered what she had said about carrying the coffee and sandwich—or was it sandwiches?

My coffee was getting cold and I said so. "I want a few minutes' breathing space and so do the rest of us, Hank," I said. "Let's forget about the murder until we've finished our lunch. I'm hungry."

He said: "You're the doctor, Nita. Let's eat." He cut me a hunk of cheese and popped it on my slice of cold toast. Then he reached for a spoonful of jam which he deposited on my paper plate.

Miss Tates mumbled something about leaving and pushed back her chair. She hastened toward the other end of the room, making for somebody who must have been near the door. In a second Marcia followed and Hank and I were left alone.

He pushed back his plate and said, looking at me: "Well, made up your mind yet?"

"I don't know what you mean. About the murderer?"

"About me."

"What is there to say? I—I rather like you, I mean. Is that what you're talking about?"

"Well, we'll call it that." He played with his coffee cup a minute. "Now let's get going on the murder business. You know you're all in the deep on this, Nita, even you."

I jumped. A sliver of cheese went down in my cup and some of the coffee splashed up on my red scarf.

"Well," he said, "take Gaines and his wife Marcia. Secretly married. A baby on the way. Gaines especially anxious to keep his job because he knows Marcia will have to give hers up soon. Then along comes ex-wife, with a story. She appears and faints. Gaines tries to keep her in the department instead of sending her to a hospital or letting her go home with one of the girls. Why? Because he was afraid of what she might say otherwise."

I remembered suddenly a look from Mary Smith to Gaines. A see-you-later look. I told Hank about it and he nodded. I remembered, too, that Gaines hadn't wanted to move her out of the department, but I had thought then that the reason he stuck close was that Mary was the kind of girl men do things for.

"Marcia and Gaines didn't do it," I told Hank. "They couldn't. They're not that kind."

"Maybe not. But here comes ex-wife with a shotgun demand. 'Give me your diamond ring'—or maybe it was money she asked for and they didn't have money, so they substituted the diamond—'or I'll find a way of proving that the divorce was illegal.'"

"Impossible," I said, trying to believe myself. "She got the divorce and she knew it was legal."

He waved my objection aside. "I've heard it said," he told me, "that any divorce could be proved illegal and non-existent if you got a crooked enough lawyer working on it long enough. Okay. Let's put it this way. She'll invalidate the divorce and therefore the remarriage unless she gets what she wants. Marcia gives her the ring, which is still on her finger when she is killed."

"That proves," I thought aloud, "that Marcia and Gaines didn't do it. Or they'd have taken off the ring so that they wouldn't be connected with the crime at all."

"There's something to that."

At that minute I saw Miss Emily coming. She sat herself down in the chair that Hank placed for her and after he had brought her some coffee and she had refused toast and cheese, she began: "You are Mr. Bemis."

Hank bowed. "Hank Bemis. Henry Bemis." I expected him to say, "Call me Hank," but he didn't.

Miss Emily put some sheets of paper on the table. "They told me," she said, "that I'd have to get your okay before the paper would run this ad. It's good, startling advertising, Mr. Bemis."

Automatically, this time, Hank murmured his "Call me Hank" line and, to my surprise, Miss Emily accepted it.

"This ad, Hank, is the first," she said, putting a layout sheet down on the table and unfolding it. The three of us peered at it.

NOT EVEN MURDER COULD STOP THIS SALE.

"That's real advertising," said Miss Emily proudly, looking at the rather straggly printing.

Maybe it wasn't orthodox advertising, but it would certainly make the customers stop, look and listen. And if they'd buy the goods after they were in the store, then it was good advertising. Or was it?

There were subheads:

WE HAD A MURDER IN OUR STORE. AN UNKNOWN WOMAN WAS KILLED THROUGH CIRCUMSTANCE BEYOND OUR CONTROL

I almost giggled at that. It was a little stiff, like some of Miss Emily's clothes, but still it went surprisingly well with the tone of the ad, which continued:

> *We'll find the murderer, with the help of our efficient police. . . .*

I looked at Hank and he looked at the layout. His ears were a little red and there was a sort of twitch at the corner of his mouth.

> *In the meantime,* said a solid paragraph in 14-point type, *we want your help. There are clues to the murder in the store. They might be anything or anywhere. A bolt of silk, a leather handbag, a pair of silk stockings. A string of beads. Anything in the store might conceal a clue to the murder.*
>
> *Come here tomorrow to do your September Sales shopping. But while you are buying, play detective. To the woman presenting the best clue, we will give a prize of $500 if she presents with her clue sales-checks that prove she has bought at least five dollars worth of goods in the store any time after today's date. To the next five women who present authentic clues, we will give prizes of a merchandise order for ten dollars and will in addition cancel their*

bills for the current month if they run between
$100 and $200.
  Come to our store and do your shopping.
  Play detective and get bargains at the same
time.

The rest of the page was taken up with items scheduled for the September Sales. I noticed with amusement that Miss Emily had added a few cents to the price of almost every item.

Hank read the thing over for the second time. When he turned to Miss Emily, I thought he looked a little dazed.

Almost reverently, he said: "You'll make money on this sale. You won't lose anything even if the store is closed today."

"Of course I'll make money. Do you think Bertram and I are in business for our health?" So Bertram was still the figurehead he had always been. I hadn't even seen him today, except for a minute or two in the general executive meeting when we were gathered for the police to question us.

"Today," said Hank sternly, "the store stays closed. All day. Maybe by tonight we'll have found the murderer."

"Good," snapped Miss Emily. "So much the better. We'll start off with a fair field. If you have the real criminal under lock and key it can't hurt the public to have its fun being detectives. And we can afford these prizes whether the clues are real clues or only some string left under a counter by the janitor."

"There's only one like you, Miss Emily," Hank said. "They broke the mold after they made you. Damned if I don't think you'll put it over. And," he added handsomely, "if we don't find the murderer in this one day, you've got a right to try your hand. I don't think," he said, turning to me, "they'll let us keep the store closed after today anyhow, so Miss Emily may just as well have her ad."

He scrawled a note on the edge of the ad sheet. "There," he said, "tell Bailey, at the *Record*, that I think it's okay. I told him in this note that it was part of the campaign to trap the murderer. That's a lie, but it might as well be the truth for all I know about the murderer."

Miss Emily carefully folded her layout sheets and went on her way. Hank sat back and howled. I liked the way his laugh rang out in the crowded lunch-room and didn't even mind the way everybody turned around to look.

I remembered what he had said when Marcia and Miss Tates were at the table and asked: "Where's your murderer? First you said you had a murderer, and then you told Miss Emily that you didn't know anything about the murderer. You're a liar either way. Which is the truth?"

"Listen, Nita, I haven't any more idea who murdered that girl than you have," he said earnestly. "I've asked questions until I'm blue in the face. I've listened to statements and looked wise, as if they meant something. I've told people things in an important voice, trying to persuade myself that I was talking sense. I've talked and listened and looked for the last three hours and I'm just where I started from. I don't know a damn thing."

"But you told Marcia and Miss Tates that you had a murderer."

"That, my dear young woman, is what is known as bluff. If any cop pounding a beat couldn't do better than I've done this morning, I'd eat my last summer's hat."

Helplessly we looked at each other. I kind of liked him helpless that way. And he had a habit of brushing his hair back untidily that made him look about sixteen.

I thought of something, and it made me feel kind of red around the ears. I asked: "Did you read my letters? I mean did you read the letters and things I tore up and stuffed into that envelope you took out of the waste-basket?"

He stared at the hunk of cheese that was left and recited in an undertone: "You're the only girl in the world. When you look at me I don't care if there are any other women anywhere."

"Crook," I berated him. "Liar!"

"I had to," he said. "I had to make sure that somebody hadn't slipped anything in there. The next time you throw away love letters, tear 'em up a little. These were just crumpled, mostly, and a few torn in half. And there was a dried rosebud and an orchid corsage that you must have worn at some time. Oh, and a left glove. And a spool of darning silk. Never throw away darning silk," he added. "You might marry a poor detective some day and need to put some new feet in the stockings you've worn for a year or two."

I hated him and said so. But he didn't seem disturbed. I knew, of course, that part of the routine of looking for murderers was examining the waste-baskets in the "murder room," as they'd probably be calling it soon. After all, maybe it was better to have Hank examine the stuff than one of the regulars of the homicide squad. Clancy, for instance. Or the one with the knowing look and the bald head.

Hank put his hand on mine. "Listen, kid," he said, "I took that stuff into the wash-room and flushed it. They'd have to search the sewers for it now. What the hell is it to me who was in love with you last year? It's this year and next year I'm bothered about. Any chance for a dumb cop in plain clothes? Or are you ad gals so swell that the police department doesn't stand a chance? you ever date on weekday nights? Today's Friday."

I felt a little lightheaded. "I'll break one any time," I said, "with or without telephoning the other guy first. I like guys who ask for dates on Fridays. And I've always liked cops since one found me when I was lost off the merry-go-round when I was six."

We had another couple of cups of hot coffee on that, and Hank, with a dreamy expression on his face, ate a piece of rather rubbery cheese.

Just about that time, Mr. Bertram Paul came. His thin hand was shaking worse than ever when he thrust a paper at me. "Look," he said. "This was on my desk."

The paper with the splotch of blood looked familiar and then I was shocked to remember that I'd seen it in Gaines' hand when we were all in the meeting and when he was taking down notes for Miss Emily just before I left the room.

In the excitement I'd forgotten to tell Hank. Maybe I hadn't intended to. Well, anyhow, he didn't know, and I did.

Carefully, with the edge of a handkerchief, Hank took the paper and read the words that were scrawled on it:

MURDER—TODAY—YOU

Just the three words. One above the blood splotch. One to the left of it, and one to the right of it. With the blood emphasizing and pointing up the words.

"I'll be the next," quavered Mr. Bertram. He was shaking with fear, and he shuddered away from the paper that Hank held.

"It's probably somebody just horsing around trying to see if you're good for a scare," Hank soothed him. But Hank was worried, too. I got that in a minute. He had a way of wrinkling between the eyebrows when he was worried.

Indignantly, Mr. Bertram glared at him. With dignity he announced: "I am the president and general manager of this store. I am the most important member of this staff. Danger to me is danger to the store. The murder of this other individual was not important. Inconvenient, but not important, except to me. But the threat to me is something that you must handle immediately and successfully."

As usual, the poor, ineffectual devil talked like a board meeting. I wondered whether he really believed that he was important to the running of the store. So far as I could tell, he never did anything but countersign checks and papers and dictate indignant letters in answer to suggestions that came to him from people who thought his title meant something. I know his secretary carried all his signed letters to Miss Emily to read before she mailed them, and Miss Emily quietly removed any that might harm the prestige of the store or anybody's opinion of Mr. Bertram.

Patiently, Hank Bemis explained everything that the police were doing, expressing a little more optimism for results than he had shown me.

"It's a swell set-up, Mr. Bertram," he said enthusiastically. "Here we are with a whole day to solve the murder, and every suspect on tap. Nobody in the store except the employees, and we can keep them the rest of the day without danger of damage suits because they are being paid to be here, anyhow. None of the few customers in the store even came upstairs, so we sent 'em home after taking their names. The search is narrowed down. We know that only ten people in the store saw this woman when she was here the day before yesterday."

Mr. Bertram looked still more frightened for a minute. I wondered why.

Hank enumerated the ten:

"Gaines and his wife, Marcia; Miss Emily; Nita Manners; Charlie, the office-boy; Miss Rebecca Allen; Agnes

Bailey, the commercial artist who was doing a fashion drawing in the office at the time Mary Smith appeared; Miss Tates, the corset buyer; the photographer, Jake Newton."

"That's nine," I reminded him.

He nodded. "And, of course," he finished calmly, "you saw her too, Mr. Bertram. Are you ready to tell me about her now?"

SIX

You could just see Mr. Bertram wilt. He never had been a big man, but now he looked more fragile than ever. He stuttered and stammered and began a few times to try to put on his pompous manner again, but this time it wouldn't work.

Then Hank asked quietly: "Was it letters? Was she blackmailing you?"

Fearfully, Mr. Bertram said: "I knew her when she was married to Gaines. I—a couple of times kissed her when I saw her and nobody was around. I think she got the divorce thinking I'd marry her. But—I couldn't. Not then—"

You could see how his habit of pompous indecision even robbed him of the love he wanted and couldn't take. I felt a little sorry for him and wished he'd shut up and give himself a chance. Yet you could see that he didn't hate the memory of this woman. He was the kind of person who could never hate a woman he had once loved, because she still held for him something of the glamour of a person who had considered him as wonderful as he hoped he was.

"You wrote letters to her?"

"I wrote letters. I—I loved her, and I told her so. Then, later, she told me that somebody had gotten hold of the letters and was demanding money. She had no money, so she came to me. I couldn't have the letters I had written in the hands of a blackmailer, so I gave her the money to give to him."

I could see it and so could Hank. Poor old devil. Just one more racket and he was the type to fall for it.

"You didn't see this punk at all?" asked Hank. "This blackmailer?"

But Mr. Bertram nodded. "Yes, I saw him. But Emily handled everything. I was too busy to be annoyed by trifles, so I went to Emily, who took all the details off my hands. I saw the man for a minute. Just to identify the letters. Emily paid over the money and everything was finished."

"Did you ever see Mary Smith again?"

"You mean Mary Paul," he said with dignity. "Mrs. Bertram Paul. She was my wife. We were married a week ago, although we had not announced it to my sister."

"Well, I'll be a so-and-so!" swore Hank. "When did you see her last?"

"She left the apartment the day before yesterday. I was a little worried. She didn't wear any of the new things I had bought her. None of her luggage was gone either. That afternoon I thought I saw her in the store, going in the direction of the advertising department. But she didn't have on any make-up and she had her hair slicked back so she looked thin and haggard. And she was poorly dressed, so I thought I'd made a mistake. At the time, though, I thought she had decided that she didn't love me any more and was going to see her first husband, Gaines. I was—annoyed."

"How did she explain why she blackmailed you?"

"She didn't blackmail me. I thought I explained. It was this man. This—punk, you called him. He stole the letters. She was as distressed as I was."

Hank and I looked at each other. "What did that punk look like?" Hank asked thoughtfully.

Mr. Bertram thought for a minute and then said: "Like Gaines, I thought. Except he had a beard and a mustache and wore dark spectacles. Rough clothes, too, but he was built like Gaines, I thought."

"Oh, no," I answered Hank's unvoiced idea. "No!"

"It's possible," Hank told me. We understood each other.

The lunch-room was still crowded. Nobody had anything else to do, so they stayed there and talked and ate and smoked, making appropriate faces at the No-Smoking signs on the walls.

Mr. Bertram pointed to the paper that Hank still held. "You'll find who did this?"

"It stands to reason that I will. Everybody who could have done it was here. The store policeman was at the employees' door. Nobody unknown came in. The customers' door was open only a minute and only three or four people came in. None of them even went up as far as the second floor. The murder happened on the seventh floor. We know who brought her the coffee the day before. We know where she hid in a washroom when the store was closed yesterday and the day before. We'll find the murderer very soon, Mr. Bertram, and when we find the murderer, we'll probably know who sent you this note—if it wasn't somebody horsing."

It all sounded so cut and dried, and yet it wasn't really that simple. I watched Mr. Bertram's fragile figure strut its way through the crowd and then turned back to Hank.

"I've something to confess. I know about that paper," I admitted.

"So you've taken up ribbing as a sideline?"

I told him about seeing it in Gaines' heap of papers and how Gaines had probably just taken down notes on the sheet without even noticing the blood spot. Because if you saw him then, you'd know. He was sort of dazed. Just taking down Miss Emily's notes about the Murder Sale on the papers—

"Listen. Could those words be in Gaines' writing? Could they be things Miss Emily dictated to Gaines about the sale?"

We grabbed a pencil and a paper from some stuff in Hank's pockets and tried to remember the copy on Miss Emily's chief ad.

It worked out near enough, MURDER—TODAY— YOU. It could have been the part that talked about *"YOU can be a detective. . . . Any time after TODAY, MURDER in our store. . . ."* Near enough. Copy doesn't always go in the papers in the same order in which it's written.

That was explained, then, and it wasn't anything so important after all. Except—

Hank said it then. "Except—who found the paper and put it on Mr. Bertram's desk?"

I remembered something else. "Look here," I said, "do you remember when Marcia came out of the cut-room after you talked to her? Gaines seemed to be faint and she ran to him."

He blushed a little. "I was looking at you," he said. "You kind of got me, giving me the cigarettes and grinning at me so nice when I borrowed your case of cigarettes. I didn't even notice Gaines."

"Well, if he fainted right then, with the paper in his hand, and he dropped the paper, anybody in the room could have picked it up and put it on Mr. Bertram's desk. Everybody on your list was there in that room."

"So helpful," he said. He put down again on a paper the names of the ten people who had seen Mary Smith. No— Mary Gaines. No—Mary Paul, Mrs. Bertram Paul. "Got any pets for the prospective murderer?" he asked.

It was just at that minute that we heard the shot. A boom that resounded through the empty corridors. I couldn't tell where it came from.

The lunch-room was a bedlam. Girls were screaming. One of them fainted. Men were yelling. And in one corner everybody was crowding out toward the door, looking into the corridor.

Hank was gone, shouldering his way through the crowd like a football player. He didn't come back at all, and I just sat there because my knees were too weak for holding me up.

Charlie came along in about ten minutes after the crowd had been cleared out of the doorway and the corridor.

"Who is it? Not Marcia?" I asked. I don't know why I thought of Marcia. But I kept being more and more afraid about Gaines, somehow. I didn't like the way he had looked at his ex-wife, and I didn't care for the fact that he had wanted to keep her at the store right under his eye.

"No, it's Mr. Bertram."

"Dead?"

"I don't know. He was still living when they picked him up. They've got him in the hospital room now, with the store nurse, and they've called back the police doctor who had already left. Maybe Mr. Bertram didn't live till he got there. I wouldn't know."

"Oh, Charlie, we didn't help him, and he asked us to," I wailed.

I found myself telling him about the piece of paper with the threat on it, and Charlie sat there beside me looking terribly young but very sympathetic. He said:

"That Hank guy likes you. He asked me what your name was, right away when he saw you. Before he ever talked to you. He said you looked like his mother, or something. I know that story. You wouldn't fall for a cop, Miss Nita, would you?"

"Why not? I made a date with him for tonight if both of us are off. Maybe they'll have us in jail."

"Not you. I saw him slipping some of your papers out and tearing 'em up. And when Clancy wanted to see 'em, he threatened to tell something on Clancy if he as much as mentioned the papers. Said they didn't have anything to do with the case and he wasn't going to have a girl's private life upset just because she happened to be working in a store where somebody was murdered."

"Good for Hank; he's a swell guy. How do I know whether I'll fall for him? I never saw him in my life before today."

"Oh, well, Miss Nita, a guy's got to get married sometime. Now look at me. Miss Nita, do you think a guy could get married if he's only eighteen? How old do you think a man ought to be before he gets married?"

He went on to ask personal advice in his usual way and I tried to pay attention to what he was saying. But I kept thinking about Mr. Bertram who had come to us for help. And we had let him go out to his death. It would have been so easy for one of us to go with him, but we were feeling so nice about being together, and besides we didn't take him seriously enough to think he was in any danger.

Now he was shot. Dead maybe.

And all because we hadn't taken him seriously enough to put him under protection. There were dozens of policemen and plain-clothes men in the place and we didn't think of getting one to protect him.

It didn't do any good to blame ourselves. Still, I knew Hank would feel the way I did about it. I knew a surprising amount about how Hank would feel about things. At least, I thought I did.

I wondered if Bertram was dead. We just sat there silently for a few minutes listening to the chatter around us.

Somebody said Mr. Bertram had been shot through the heart and was dead when they picked him up. Somebody else said he was shot through the head and died instantly. Others said it was just his arm or his shoulder, and only a flesh wound at that. I hoped the last statement was true, but I had no way of finding out. They had policemen on guard at the corridor doors, keeping us out of the way so they could make further investigations.

Locking the stable door after the horse was gone, I kept thinking.

Charlie didn't say much, but he seemed uneasy. Finally he asked: "Miss Nita, if you know something about a murder and don't tell, can they arrest you and put you in jail?"

"I think they call it accessory after the fact, or something like that, Charlie. I'm not sure. What do you know?"

"Well, I'll tell you. In the first place, I saw another sandwich and another bottle of coffee. Only this time they were all new. The coffee was warm and the bottle full. The sandwich was still wrapped in paper. They had been on a little ledge behind the couch in the photographer's studio. Jake found them first and he started to eat the sandwich and drink the coffee. But when I asked him he looked scared and said he'd found them there. He showed me the place. He said somebody had left them there and he didn't know who."

"I know about that," I told him gently. "Hank knows who brought the stuff in for the woman. He doesn't know why yet."

But Charlie still looked frightened. "Listen," he said, "Jake was sick as hell up in the studio. They've got somebody up there washing out his stomach and giving him antidotes. And he only had a little of the coffee and a bite of the sandwich. Lucky he didn't eat it all."

"Oh, no—no—he wasn't—the stuff wasn't—poisoned?"

But Charlie nodded miserably. "It was, though. They were just sending me to get Hank—Mr. Bemis. To tell him about it and get him up there. It all just happened. I left Betty here and went up there. I thought I'd see if anybody had brought food to Mary Smith like yesterday. So I could *tell* them whether she spent the night here. And when I got there Jake was just opening the stuff and starting to eat it. It all happened right away. Everything. And—I found this."

With a face that looked more and more miserable, Charlie held out to me a crisp white handkerchief of the kind of linen that Miss Tates brings back from her New York trips. She buys them at a little Chinese place and uses them for jabots and for dress trimmings as well as for handkerchiefs.

"Nobody else has any handkerchiefs like this, Miss Nita. I guess Miss Tates did it. And she shouldn't have, because Jake likes her a lot."

"Jake?"

"The photographer. The only one who knew—besides me—that Mary Smith must have spent the night in the studio. Because he told me to change the couch-cover and it was only the couch-cover that proved that she'd been here all night. Otherwise that hair might have come from the first time she was on the couch. Miss Tates tried to kill Jake, the photographer, Miss Nita, and next she'll try to kill me."

SEVEN

They asked us questions about where we were when these two attempted murders had happened, and I saw that Hank's face was worn and haggard, as if he were blaming himself for what had happened to Mr. Bertram.

We didn't get a chance to talk to each other. Lane was allowed to help with the questions this time, and he had his troubles.

Miss Emily was complaining because the papers flatly refused to print the ad she had concocted and talked about respect for the law and all that sort of thing. But about that time, Miss Emily pulled her threat about cancelling her newspaper contracts and using direct mail only and so they agreed to print the ad if the police department okayed it. The police department did. I don't know how officially it was done, but at any rate Hank phoned somebody at each of the papers and pretty soon we began to hear the newsboys selling extras on the streets. There were crowds standing around the store, and across the street people were staring up. Of course the police kept them moving, but still it looked like a parade.

Reporters were trying to get in, too, and calling on the phone, and every once in a while the phone would ring and it would be one of the newspaper boys I know, trying to get some stories on the side from me. I know a lot of the boys. You get to know 'em, in the advertising business.

Miss Emily was in her glory, once the papers were on the street with her ad in them. She didn't even seem too upset about Mr. Bertram. She took the news of his marriage quite calmly, it seemed to me. It began to occur to me that Miss Emily herself could be the murderer we were looking for. So far as motive is concerned, she might have wanted to get rid of Mary to keep her from marrying Mr. Bertram. It didn't sound likely, but there was always a chance.

Miss Emily went in two or three times to the hospital room to see Mr. Bertram, and the last time she came out she was furious.

"The idea of him lying there and letting all these policemen tear up the store this way when he should be on his feet doing a job himself!" she said. "He's no more sick than I am. The doctor says it's only a flesh wound. Just a scratch that bled a little. They've got him strapped up like a wounded soldier, but there's nothing much wrong with him. He could put the arm in a sling and come out and help, if he's capable of helping, which I doubt. But he might give us moral support, anyhow."

Mr. Willing, the shoe buyer, tittered in his usual fashion, and Jake, who had recovered from his slight attack of poisoning, managed a laugh. Both of them seemed to know Mt. Bertram well. Jake looked green, I thought. "Just enough poison to be uncomfortable," he said. "They washed out my stomach and here I am, good as new and twice as handsome."

I began to get shivery as I listened to one question after another and knew that the murderer must be somewhere among us. By this time, they'd practically exonerated the general personnel of the store—salesgirls, models and office help. Elevator people, too, and all the odds and ends of extras. They'd given them a half holiday and sent them home.

The search was narrowing and it horrified me a little. Mr. Willing kept tittering about the things that had happened, as if they were something funny instead of stark tragedy. I knew it was only nervousness, but it didn't make it any easier to stand, and Marcia said, under her breath: "If somebody had to be killed, why couldn't it have been him."

Then she suddenly realized what she was saying and got a little pale. As I saw her lean back in her chair I felt a little afraid for her. After all, she was having a baby and murder investigations aren't supposed to be the most wonderful tonic in the world for prospective mothers.

I heard some people talking behind us and looked around to see Mr. Bertram, all done up in bandages and a sling for his arm. He was talking to Miss Emily and Miss Tates and Jake, and I don't think they heard what Marcia said. At least, I didn't think so then. Later on, I wasn't so sure.

Mr. Bertram was telling his story all over again for the benefit of everybody in the room. He had just said: "And the shot came from nowhere. They found the gun right beside me. Whoever used it must have thrown it. But they didn't find a clue."

"Finger-prints?" asked Miss Tates, anxiously.

Mr. Bertram shook his head. "No. Only mine, where I picked it up. Somebody said, 'There's the gun.' I was only half-conscious and I picked it up."

He seemed entirely to have forgotten his wife's death in his excitement and pride over his own shooting. He seemed to be enjoying it thoroughly and it wasn't hard to see why. It had been a long time since he was the central figure in anything, as he was in this shooting. Even Jake, with his poisoning, didn't stand a chance. The police doctor had told Jake that he had taken so little of the stuff that he didn't have much more than an upset stomach, and that he probably would be all right in another hour or two, although he was lucky that he'd stopped eating when he did. They hadn't tested the poison yet, or at any rate, we hadn't heard what they found.

Hank finished asking questions and came up to me. He looked terribly tired, I thought. "We're well out of those things," he said, nodding toward Mr. Bertram and again at Jake. "We could easily have had three corpses on our hands today."

"You look tired," I told him.

"And well I might, lady. With three murders, or would-be's, in one day and nothing like a good, long drink of anything to cool the old brain."

"We could send out," I told him. "Charlie knows the way to the liquor store and they sell sandwiches in the delicatessen at the corner? Like the idea?"

"Now I know I like you," he said, and went in search of Charlie.

I was a little scared when we sat down in a corner of the cut-room. The two other attempts had happened when we were together and I felt a little afraid that something more might happen while we were here. But everything went smoothly.

Except when Charlie came in with a long face to say that he was sorry he had accused Miss Tates of trying to poison Jake and of wanting to poison him, too. The police had decided by that time that the poisoned coffee or sandwich—whichever it was—had been intended for Mary Paul. Either the murderer had planned to use the poison and then, in a passion, had chosen the shears as quicker, or two different people had been laying for her. Nobody knew which.

Mr. Willing came in and made himself obnoxious by teasing us about the ad-maid and the policeman. And Miss Emily came to make a few suggestions about a follow-up ad for the first of the week. But after that we had our long, cool drinks and the world looked a little better.

Hank said: "If Bertram had died after I laughed at him instead of helping him, I'd never have looked at anybody again."

"It wasn't your fault. He's a nut. How were you to know that he wasn't just crazy?"

"Well, his wife had been killed. He had a warning. Look here, Nita, have you gone to my head? Just because I meet a girl do I have to forget the first fundamentals about police procedure?"

"There you go, blaming it all on me," I said.

"Well—isn't it your fault?"

Mr. Willing came back about that time, to put in an objection about the shoe cut in Monday's ad. While we were changing to the murder ad, couldn't we find time to make a new shoe cut? I said we would if we could, not having the slightest intention of doing it, and pretended I didn't notice the wink his left eye gave me as I shut the door behind him.

"Some day somebody's going to kill that guy," I said, "and I'm not going to weep any tears about it."

Later I remembered saying that. But for half an hour Hank and I tried to forget Mr. Willing and just talked about possibilities, trying to get along into the murder without being too personal. It was good, but not too helpful. But we did enjoy it, being together.

Then Hank went back to work and I sat on a stool in the cut-room and tried to write the follow-up ad on a table only half big enough for my layout sheet. They wouldn't let me have a typewriter because they were all in the murder room. So I had to write my copy out longhand and pray that the printer wouldn't refuse to try to make it out.

Not that any printer would really refuse to work on an ad like this. He'd be pleased as Punch just to be able to say to his friends: "Did you see that ad—that murder ad? Well, I made it up, and it took some work, too. Why, the whole damned thing was written out in longhand." I could just hear him.

Hank poked his head in the door twice, once to ask if I'd seen Lane, the store detective, and once to ask what time the store opened in the morning on Saturdays. That was Friday.

A little later Lane came to the door that led into the murder room and opened it. The room was empty.

All their measuring and photographing and cleaning was done. They had gone over everything, including my desk. I discovered later that there was a run in a new pair of silk stockings that I'd left in a box in my top drawer, to use in any emergency. You get stocking emergencies when you work at an old rolltop desk with the splinter habit.

Lane said: "I guess it's all right to get anything off your desk now, Miss Nita. Do you know that they even vacuum clean a room? Did you hear 'em? They just went over everything. Anybody would think they was hunting for grains of dust."

I didn't go into the room, and didn't even look in except to notice that everything was orderly except for the chalk line on the floor. I found out about the silk stockings later.

Lane brought me my pencils and a stack of copy paper and I stayed in the cut-room. I didn't take my typewriter because somebody else was using it. Well, the printer could fight about the copy, if he wanted to.

There I was, paying strict attention to my own business, when Miss Tates came in. She was puffing a little as if she had been running and I could see that she had been crying, too. Her ruffles weren't as fresh and crisp as usual and she dabbed her eyes with one of her Chinese handkerchiefs. I wondered if Charlie had given back to her the one that he had found.

She had just found herself a seat on the edge of a table when Miss Rebecca Allen came hurrying in and went straight to her.

"Belle," she said, in a tone of affection I hadn't ever heard her use to anybody else, "have you forgiven me?"

At Miss Rebecca's words, Miss Tates again burst into tears.

EIGHT

I wanted to crawl in a hole and pull the hole in after me.
I felt I didn't have the right to listen in on a personal
conversation like this. But pretty soon it filtered through
my dense head that almost everything that happened today was important to me and to the store because of the
murder. Important to Hank, too, and that made quite a
difference, somehow.

So I listened. It was all about a diary and about something that had been written in it. It seemed to be Miss Rebecca's diary, but the story in it was about something that
had happened to Miss Tates when she and Miss Rebecca
went to New York together last year.

I had taken my papers back in the corner so they
wouldn't notice me especially, but now, all of a sudden,
they turned around and saw me and both of them pounced
on me at once.

Miss Rebecca said sharply: "I guess you'll tell your
boy friend about this. It isn't enough that that little snip
should carry off my diary, but the whole police department must be reading it and laughing over it."

"I didn't know—" I began. But then I stopped because I
did know. Mary Smith—Mary Paul had carried off Rebecca's diary and it had probably been discovered and handed
over to the police.

"She had it hidden under the couch-cover. She was eating peanut brittle while she read it," Miss Rebecca was saying. "It was amusement to her. She probably just carried it off to be nasty. And she read it to laugh at."

"Oh, Becky," wailed Miss Tates, "why did you write it into your diary? Why couldn't you let it be a secret? I told you everything was over between us and that he and I were only going to be friends from that time on. Why did you have to put it into your diary for her to find?"

"I'm sorry. I'm so sorry. I never thought anybody would ever see the diary but me, Belle. Honest, I didn't. And then that little snip carried it off with my best dress and my new nightgown and those shoes that Will ordered for me in New York that time for a thank-you gift because I—"

She seemed to notice me all of a sudden and she broke off, blushing, and started all over again to apologize while I tried to find out the connection between Miss Rebecca and Mr. Willing. Or was it Miss Tates who had been Mr. Willing's girlfriend? It was all too much for me. And none of my business anyhow.

At any rate, the worst thing seemed to be not that Mary had carried the diary away, but that she had left it under the cover on the couch where she had slept, and that she had been eating peanut brittle and had spilled sticky, crinkly crumbs of it in the book.

I had finished the follow-up ad. There wasn't much fresh copy except the headlines, so I got it all ready for the paper and went out in search of Charlie, hoping to see Hank, too, somewhere around.

The store looked strange that day. It never did seem completely real to me again, after that. The morning had been both terrible and exciting, while the afternoon was a lot of hell mixed up with a thin thread of wonderful minutes with this man I had just met, but who seemed so terribly important almost from the beginning.

Well, thinking about it didn't make it seem any more real. I got hold of Charlie. He was running an elevator for Hank and having a swell time doing it. He hated to stop to run over to the newspaper offices, but it was Friday and the copy for the Monday papers had to be in soon if I was to see proofs on Saturday. There wouldn't be any too much time. I knew we'd be rushed to death in the store on Saturday with this Murder Sale.

Miss Emily has theories about the people who write her advertising spending some time selling behind the counters, just to get the feel of the merchandise. I knew she'd pick on the Murder Sale Day as one of the behind-the-counter days for the ad department. Which was just as well. I needed to be brought back to earth. Any girl, I thought, who could reach the age of twenty-five without having any more sense than to fall for a detective who's on a case nearby should have her head examined.

Reluctantly, Charlie left the elevator and I took it on.

Yes, I know how to run an elevator. Miss Emily taught me how. She knows how to do everything about a store from scrubbing the floors and dressing the windows to writing the ads and buying the merchandise.

I ran the buyers up and down and stopped to talk to all of them. I hadn't seen many of them except from a distance today. Mr. Willing, the shoe buyer, and Miss Tates, the corset buyer, had been hanging around the advertising department or the lunch-room all day, but the rest had been conspicuous by their absence.

Each had his own pet theory as to the identity of the murderer. The hat buyer insisted that a tramp had come in from the outside and hidden and done all the damage. She was so sure about him that she could almost have sworn to the color of his eyes. I hated to destroy her illusions, so I didn't say much and didn't even raise my eyebrows very high, but she could see that I didn't believe very strongly in her theories. The dress buyer, Ken Lang, insisted that it was one or another of the porters or scrub-women or even a stock-girl. "It stands to reason," he said, "that anybody who wanted to hide would take on the personality of a colorless individual like a porter."

The neckwear and lace buyer, who is something of a card, suggested dryly that some people might consider buyers the most colorless individuals around a department store.

The underwear buyer, one of those clinging women, a little too old for clinging, and too angular, gushed all over the place about how terribly "fwightened" she was, all for the benefit of Mr. Henderson, the hosiery and leather goods buyer, who was in the elevator at the time. He winked at me behind her back, but she saw him in the elevator mirror and got out at the seventh floor with a sniff and a catty remark that I pretended not to hear.

Hank got in on one trip, looking very tired. He brightened when he saw me. "So this is where you've got to," he said. "I thought I gave Charlie this job."

"You did, but I sent him to the paper with an ad, so I took his place till he came back."

"Good," he said. "I'll run it, too. I know how."

I stepped aside to give him my place and he skillfully ran it up a floor and a half, then down a piece, and stopped between floors.

I was a little frightened and jumped for the wheel. But he held out his arm to stop me. "I have the elevator trained," he said. "It stops or goes, just as I want it to. Now come here. I want to show you something."

He put his arms around me and I felt him tremble a little. He bent his head and his lips touched my cheek.

"Damn crowd," he muttered. "Can't get your girl alone. There! I've been wanting to do that all day."

He didn't really kiss me. Not a regular kiss. But somehow I liked it better this way. He started the elevator again and we went up, then he got out and left the elevator to me.

After Charlie got back, I rode with him a few times, talking to the rest of the buyers as they went up and down, and to Miss Emily, and Mr. Bertram, who still had his arm in its sling and was all puffed up with his own importance.

I was still in the elevator when the next murder happened. It still makes me shudder to say it like that, quick and matter-of-fact.

I had just taken Miss Emily up and was still standing with my hand on the wheel—it wasn't really a wheel, of course, but we called it that. It was then that I heard Miss Tates scream. "Will!" she was calling. "Will!" And then just one fierce scream after another. Shrill. Horrible.

The sounds seemed to come from the second floor in the new shoe salon, and I slipped the elevator down to that floor, but just as I was stopping it, somebody gave me a call from seven, where I'd last taken Hank, so I went back. It was Hank, all right. He said:

"It came up through the radiator. Did you hear it?"

"Second floor," I told him. "The shoe salon. It's Miss Tates' voice yelling for Mr. Willing."

We didn't waste time talking, and Hank was out of the car before I could say anything more. Miss Tates was still yelling. I could hear her. And then I heard Miss Rebecca. She was crying at the top of her voice, with a sort of shrill, hopeless sound.

I don't suppose I should have left the elevator. There were calls now from all over. But I saw one of the porters lumbering along with a trash-basket. It was old Frank who had been an elevator operator on the old cars before we put girls on.

I called him and asked him whether he could still run
a car and he sort of looked me up and down as if I'd asked
a college professor whether he knew his A B C's. He took
over, fondling the wheel as proudly as a mother pushing a
baby carriage with twins in it.

He went up on a call and I went on into the shoe salon,
following Hank. It was Willing, of course.

He was slumped down in a heap, with open boxes of
new shoes around him, and a nasty little knife was sticking
out of his back.

"You can almost see how it happened," Hank said. "He
was sitting down here, on the floor, studying these new
shoes that have just come in. It's the best way to pile up
all the stuff this way and be able to get at it. You can see
that. Somebody came up behind him on this soft carpet
and gave him just one swift jab."

Miss Tates moaned a little. "Oh, no!" she kept spying.
"Oh, Will! Oh, no!"

I started to go to her, but Hank motioned me back.
"Stay back there, all of you," he said. "This carpet is lousy
with footprints already. We probably can't tell anything.
But stay away, anyhow. You can't help him and you may
hinder us getting the murderer."

His face looked a little gray, I thought, and his voice
didn't sound indifferent or tough. You'd think a detective
who'd been a policeman would get used to things like that,
but he took it almost as hard as I did. I kept my eyes on
him instead of on Mr. Willing's face.

By this time the rest of the gang had gathered. Everybody was crowding up the steps and out of the elevator
and although I'd thought the store was practically empty
it was still crowded enough to be bewildering.

Hank said things to several policemen who were there
and the work began. They herded the buyers and the rest
of the lookers into the next room, where we sold the junior

shoes and left Mr. Willing alone, sprawled on the blue carpet in the shoe salon he had been so proud of.

Annoying as Mr. Willing had always been to me, I couldn't help wondering how anybody could kill a man who so obviously enjoyed life. I remembered saying earlier in the day that I wouldn't waste any tears on his death, yet I found my eyes smarting with tears of horror at the sight of the sprawling figure. I remembered that Marcia had said something of the same sort, too, earlier in the afternoon, and I kept wondering whether anybody had heard her and acted on what she had said. Or even—if she had dared to act on her own advice.

This was ridiculous. I was like all the rest of them. I would accuse anybody. Even Marcia. Why, I'd even found myself suspecting Miss Emily, whom I adored, in spite of her little tricks, and ineffectual Mr. Bertram, and Mr. Gaines who'd been the grandest advertising manager to work with I'd ever known. That's what suspicion will do to an otherwise sane mind.

It seems to me that we spent most of our time that day waiting around to be questioned. Not answering questions. Because there didn't seem to be much to be answered.

I made list after list for Hank, telling him where I'd taken everybody. I found myself remembering with startling accuracy where everybody had gone. But plenty of the people still in the store had walked up and down the stairs and there just didn't seem to be any way of accounting for any of them. We tried methods of trying to make out comparative time charts showing where everybody was at any time. But it didn't work. Everybody was wandering around and nobody seemed to have any accurate watches, and the clocks of the store seemed to be hidden behind September Sale posters or banners. And poor Hank just kept on poking more and more frenzied.

The police doctor looked rather cross. "Look," he said, "can't you sort of lump your corpses? I've been coming and going here all day. Two half ways and a couple of completes. Let's hope this is the last call for today."

He wouldn't make any statement except to say that Willing hadn't been dead more than twenty minutes, which would make the time of death practically simultaneous with Miss Tates' first scream.

Miss Tates said that she had come on him just as he was falling. That she thought he had fallen asleep or had slipped over a shoe box or something. Then, when she came nearer, she saw the knife.

There was very little blood. The clothes had apparently soaked up what little there was. Internal bleeding, the doctor said, and emphasized the excellent aim and trained strength of the person who had done the job.

He even seemed a little proud of the way it was done. Kept repeating: "A beautiful thing. A beautiful thing."

And he wouldn't commit himself about whether it took a lot of strength or only a lot of skill in addition to the very sharp knife.

The homicide squad men got back on the job again. The time before I'd only heard them, but this time I saw them at work. The terrible thing it seemed to me was that they went about the business so methodically. They took pictures as casually as if they were making still life photographs for murals.

They went through all the papers on the desk and in the waste-basket. They photographed and measured and examined. They put tapes with things written on them around Mr. Willing's wrist. They even took his finger-prints and went around testing for other finger-prints. Of course they found dozens, in a place like a store, and that seemed for some reason to make them angry. As if we hadn't done right by them not to let them have the finger-prints they

wanted without getting them mixed up with those of customers and salespersons.

About that time I couldn't stand it any longer and I
went out just when some men came in with a big basket.
That was the last straw. I sat down rather suddenly in a
corner and didn't do anything for a little while.

Marcia came over and sat by me and took my hand. I
was glad to see that she was looking a little better, and
said so.

"Now they can't think that my Fritz is the murderer,"
she said, triumphantly, "because he was with me every
minute of the last hour."

NINE

That seemed to put Gaines and Marcia out of the running entirely, for this last murder. They seemed to have been sitting on the seventh floor steps, talking over things. Deciding that the thing to do was to tell Marcia's mother of their marriage and then announce it to the rest of the world, even if Marcia would have to stay with her mother as long as she lived, which would probably not be more than a few weeks now.

But it was about that time when I realized that Marcia had taken off the Schiaparelli outfit and the store costume jewelry and was wearing her own neat blue suit with its crisp white blouse.

I didn't like to ask questions, but if I didn't, the police would. And my questions would be easier than the police's. Even Hank's. Hank was listening from behind me when I asked the question:

"When did you change your things, Marcia? How long did it take you?"

She whitened a little. She said: "I need a tight girdle now to make the Schiaparelli fit and I couldn't stand it a minute longer. But I was only gone fifteen minutes. The rest of the time I was with Fritz on the steps."

She knew then, that the fifteen minutes was enough to take the heart out of her alibi for Fritz. He or anybody else could easily have done the job in much less time than that. If, indeed, they would take Marcia's word for his alibi, if he had one. After all, she was his wife.

So there we were where we'd started from, with everybody in the place a suspect. I still had a few qualms about Miss Emily. Mr. Bertram and Jake were out of it, because they'd just escaped being victims themselves. But Miss Rebecca Allen, Miss Tates, the dress and coat buyers, the neckwear buyer, the hosiery and leather goods buyer, and all the rest had been in the place, and you couldn't help suspecting them.

Now we'd have to find the connection between the four murders, because of course we'd have to handle the attempts as if they had been successful. It certainly wasn't the murderer's fault that he was only 50 per cent successful.

The connections were hard to find. Mary Paul and Bertram were husband and wife. That made an easy connection there. Anybody who wanted to kill one could easily have a reason for wanting to kill the other. And Jake might have been poisoned by mistake, by somebody who thought he was poisoning food left for Mary Paul.

But Willing? That was the odd number, unless he had seen something that made him know about the other murder or the two attempted murders. For one thing, there was some sort of connection between Willing and Miss Tates, and Mary Paul knew about it from Miss Rebecca's diary. Miss Tates had brought the food to Mary Paul. She might have put in the poison that was meant for Mary and that actually was taken by Jake. Maybe Willing knew about that, so she had to kill him.

In one way all this sounded logical. In another it wasn't logical at all. Because anybody could see from the way Miss Tates acted with Willing that she was ga-ga about him, even if she did tell Miss Rebecca they were only friends now.

That's the point where we were when Hank beckoned me out into the stairway hall, closed the door behind us and sat down on the step. I sat down, too. He was leaning back against the wall and looked plenty sober.

"Well, Nita," he said, "you tell it to me. I don't know anything. They might as well give me a kiddie-car and a set of blocks and set me to playing kindergarten. I don't know anything and I can't kid myself."

I didn't know then that Hank was always that way on a case. Dismal until the last minute when everything fell into line. Sure that he was never going to get his murderer until he had the handcuffs on his wrists, or the confession signed.

Hank was the original long-faced pessimist about his work, and it took me a long time to realize it. The only time I can remember hearing him sound optimistic was when he was trying to put over a bluff on somebody and then he didn't do it particularly well. He always slumped back as soon as his audience was gone.

So when I saw him so down-hearted I really thought there was a lot to be down-hearted about. I didn't know then that he was on the right track, or thought he was.

I told him: "You'll get him yet."

"Yeah. After he's got the rest of the store killed off. I'm just lucky he hadn't tried to get you."

"You mean I'm lucky."

"Well, what do we know? It isn't this one and it isn't that. I've got reasons for knowing that it isn't anybody around the place, except maybe you and Charlie, and I know it can't be either of you. Yet nobody came in from outside. Therefore, there weren't any murders and the little princess woke up to find it was all a bad dream. If I don't get fired on this job it won't be because I don't de-serve it," he said. Then he added, "It might be anybody. Tates?"

I thought myself that she was a likely bet, so I said: "Maybe. But why?"

"Well, Mary Paul got something on Tates from Rebecca Allen's diary," he suggested. "And Tates brought the food in and later poisoned it. Then Mary decided she wasn't hungry and Tates saw your shears and used 'em. What do you think of that?"

"Go on."

"Then Jake ate the poisoned food before Tates could grab it again, and Mary had told her husband the dirt out of the diary. So Tates shot him with a pistol from the sporting goods department. Then Willing saw her do the shooting and accused her of the other murder and attempted murder, so she killed him with a hunting knife—also from the sporting goods department—in spite of the fact that she loved him. How's that?" he suggested dismally.

I knew he didn't believe it even when he was concocting it, but I said heartily:

"Swell. It's the best idea I've heard yet. Far more logical than any other."

"Oh, I'm full of ideas like that," he said mockingly. "I can tell 'em about all the inmates. I know how Miss Emily killed the girl to have a new idea for her sale, and killed Willing because he wanted to feature evening shoes instead of suit shoes, tried to shoot her brother because he was a nuisance around the store, and Jake because she wanted a new photographer and couldn't fire him because he has a long contract."

I thought I was supposed to laugh, so I did. Hank kept on getting grimmer and grimmer. "I had another idea a while ago, about Willing killing—that's a rhyme—about Willing killing Mary because she told him what a bore he was, and then just keeping up the good work because he got the habit. But I ran into trouble. Because he'd have to commit suicide then if he died at all, and men don't stick hunting knives in their own backs, even if the knives are the sharpest things out of an operating room."

"Listen, Hank, you're nutty," I said. "Send out for another drink, or run around the block and get some fresh air or something."

"Take my kiddie-car and ride, you mean. Yeah I had ideas about Jake and Bertram faking their half-killings so as to get away with the murders. And Gaines and Marcia plotting the whole business and being super-fiends or something. Oh, I'm great on these little ideas. Maybe you don't want to date with me, after all. I'm no great shakes as a cop."

I told him that he was too late, as I'd already broken a date with a newspaper reporter, but even that didn't cheer him up.

He went on to tell me a few dozen other ways in which various people might have done the job, but none of them sounded like much to me or to him either.

So we just sat there. Then he straightened up and said surprisingly: "Thanks for helping me, Nita. We'll work swell together. What'll we do tonight?"

I was a little shocked at first. It hadn't occurred to me that you could have regular dates, with deaths in stores and everything. But then I realized that death was part of Hank's business and if he called off a date every time he went on a murder case his path would be strewn with numerous broken dates.

Just about that time, the stair doorway opened and Mr. Bertram came into the hall, looking as puffed up as ever. He said:

"Several important matters have come up that I'd like to attend to outside the store, Mr. Bemis. They tell me that you must give me your okay before I attend to my own business. I consider this ridiculous."

Hank didn't say anything. He just sat there and looked up at Mr. Bertram and I could see him getting angry. He said coolly:

"And who the hell are you that you have a right to break police rules? If you kick against sticking here I'll get a warrant for your arrest in connection with the murders."

"You don't mean that you are accusing me!" Mr. Bertram was slightly purple, and then he got terribly white.

"No. But I won't have you wandering around town spilling off your mouth. Either you stay here until we have this business solved or you spend the night in the hoosegow, and damned if I care much which it is."

Mr. Bertram went out more quickly than he came in. Hank said: "I couldn't get any warrant. I haven't evidence enough to get a warrant to hold a flea. That guy doesn't know any more about the murders than Charlie does. But I've got to throw a good scare into him or he'll spoil all the plans I've made."

I didn't see any plans. All I saw was a tired-looking guy with kind of nice eyes and slim, long hands. He just seemed to sit and ask questions.

Oh, he'd been running around the place all day, but he didn't seem to be getting anywhere much. He went through all the motions, but he didn't seem to be any too sure that he was accomplishing anything. Still, detectives don't get promotions just from sitting and acting lazy. So Hank must have more sleuth sense than he acknowledged having.

And even Clancy seemed to regard him with a lot of respect. Clancy was the policeman with the notebook and the stub of a pencil in his hamlike hands.

"Listen, kid," said Hank. "Got a cigarette?"

"You have my case."

He opened it. It was empty. With a sigh he dragged out a package of papers and a yellow oilskin pack of tobacco and began to roll one of his ragged cigarettes. He gave me one and we sat there smoking awhile and saying nothing much. Once Hank shifted his cigarette to one side of his mouth and said indistinctly:

"Of course, there could be two murderers. One who finished the job on Willing and Mary Paul. And one who went off kind of half-cocked on Bertram and Jake."

I nodded. I was having trouble with flakes of tobacco on my lipstick.

"It isn't likely," he said, and sighed again.

After the second cigarette, he said, rolling the third: "Poison sounds like a woman. Maybe Tates did that, and somebody else did the others."

"Maybe."

"It all comes back to Gaines," he said. "What I don't like is that man who looked like Gaines. The one Bertram saw, with Mary. At the time the blackmail money was paid. That sounds suspicious."

"But he's crazy about Marcia. What would he be doing with Mary?"

"After all, he married Mary—once," Hank suggested.

"Yes, but Marcia—"

"Well, maybe Marcia didn't have anything to do with it. Maybe she doesn't know anything about it. Maybe he was still mixed up with his first wife, helping her get money out of Bertram, and he wanted to get rid of her to be free to announce his marriage to Marcia. Maybe that's why he killed Mary Paul and tried to kill Bertram. Because they were the only ones who could connect him with the blackmailing. Besides, he wanted to get rid of the ex-wife, anyhow."

"But Miss Emily saw the man, too," I objected. "Bertram says so."

"No, he doesn't. He said Emily handled it; that he saw the man and identified the letters. But for all we know

Emily handled it through Mary Paul. Emily won't talk.
Short of putting her through the rubber hose game I don't
see how we can make that old girl talk when she doesn't
want to. You tell me how, if you know," he added.

I didn't know how; and I said so. We sat there a while,
then Hank said: "Well, this isn't paying the preacher or
buying the ring. Back to the treadmill for me."

He helped me up and we went on out into the shoe
salon where the men were still working. Their job seemed
endless and I wanted to get away as soon as I could. I
went back to the elevator, but old Frank was having such
a good time running it that I hadn't the heart to take it
away again, so I decided to stop off at the moderate price
dress section and pick out a dress for our date tonight. I
knew the buyer would let me take it home now and put it
on my bill tomorrow.

Frank took me up and beamed at me. There was one
perfectly happy person in spite of all the murders. I wondered if we didn't have a freight elevator that he could run
somewhere in the place.

I was in the dress section when Ken Lang, the buyer,
came up.

He said: "You don't want any of that cheap stuff, Nita.
You'll get tired of it in a week."

"Listen, Lang," I told him, "if it's anything like that
chiffon I bought at the January Sale, it won't last a week.
Why don't you buy clothes that wear?"

"Because it won't do for clothes to wear too long. Nobody'll buy any new ones," he told me, grinning.

He picked out a couple of copies of more expensive
dresses and one swell little number that had been marked
down from $45 to $10.95 because it was that shade of
green-yellow that few women can wear, though it makes
me look my best. I grabbed it and a black triple-sheer
Bemberg and took them into a fitting-room to try on.

I saw the Schiaparelli outfit that Marcia had worn hanging on the rack and I thought I'd try that one on, too. It might be a little tight and it was certainly too expensive for a copywriter, but I wanted to see how I'd look in it anyhow.

The yellow dress was right and I decided to take it. I could change the clip and mend the place on the sleeve myself without any trouble. The Bemberg wasn't becoming, because the waistline was up around the neck somewhere. Only a beanpole could wear a dress like that without looking fat.

So I tried on the Schiaparelli and caught my hair on something in the belt. I went up close in front of the mirror to see what it was and discovered that somebody had fastened something inside the belt with a safety-pin.

TEN

I got the safety-pin untangled from my hair finally, took the dress off again and turned it inside out to look.

Pinned inside the belt was the amethyst ring that Marcia had worn this morning. I couldn't help noticing that some blood had seeped down in between the marcasite mounting and the stone. It looked like rust-stains at first, but marcasite doesn't rust.

I studied it for a minute, sick.

Then I put on my own dress again and went out into the department. "Mr. Lang," I said, "I'm taking this yellow-green number. Get one of the girls to put $10.95, minus my discount, on my account in the morning."

We squabbled in a friendly fashion about whether I was entitled to discount at all on a reduced dress, and then I went back upstairs. I had the ring tucked into my blouse, firmly fastened with its safety-pin.

I had to find Marcia right away. Probably I'd never wear the dress I'd bought. Just to look at it brought back the sickish feeling I'd had when I saw the ring with its bloodstain.

Marcia was in the cut-room, crying, with Gaines' arms around her.

"Fritz, Fritz," she was saying, "it'll never be the same again. Never."

And his voice, when he answered her, sounded unlike any I had ever heard from him before.

"We'll never get out of it, darling," he said. "But if we go out, we go out together."

I walked in on them then, feeling cruel and frightened all at once. Marcia gave a little moan when she saw the ring that I unfastened from my blouse.

She sat down on the stool in front of the cut-case and held out her hand for it. "All right," she said, "I'll have to tell you now, and your Hank, too. You'd better get him."

Charlie poked his head in the door and I sent him for Hank, who came in and shut the door, leaving Charlie roaming around outside waiting for things to happen. Marcia gave Hank the ring and said:

"I expected somebody to see this and nobody did. And then I got scared and put it away in the belt of my dress, where Nita found it."

Hank's lean hand went out for the ring and his lips puckered into a whistle. He said quietly: "Did you kill her?"

Marcia was more composed now than she had been all day. It seemed as if she had been fearing this all the time and now that it had come she wasn't afraid any more.

"No. But I saw her. This morning. Before she died. And later, when she was dead. That's how the blood got in the ring. I got some on my hand and washed the hand. But I didn't notice the blood on the ring until later. Nobody else noticed it, either."

"Tell me, Marcia," Hank said gently.

Gaines spoke harshly: "You shan't bedevil her. My wife—"

Gaines had his arm around her now and she leaned against his shoulder. She smiled at him maternally, then turned to Hank, saying:

"You know that we are married. Well, a few days ago Mary came here. Fritz hadn't seen her for a couple of years. Nobody here had ever known her except Mr. Bertram and Miss Emily, and Miss Tates."

"Not Miss Rebecca?"

"No. She was East when Mary and Fritz were married. And the marriage didn't last. Few people ever knew about it. Fritz didn't even tell me because he was afraid I wouldn't want to marry him if he'd been married before."

"I couldn't bear to lose her," Fritz Gaines said.

"Well, we are married, and we were so happy. I have been worried about my mother who is ill. But there isn't any hope any more. Most of the time she's in pain and I know it will be better for her when everything is over. But we didn't tell her about our marriage. I wanted to stay with her and we didn't want to make her unhappy by having her feel that she was separating us. That's the only reason for our secret."

"Let me tell it. You go and lie down, darling," Fritz said.

"No. I can stand it. Well, Mary came. She put it over on everybody. Fritz didn't know she had married again. She came in first when Fritz was alone in the office and everybody was at lunch. She wanted money. At least she said that Fritz would have to marry her again or give her money. She found out about me, somehow. Then Fritz got her out of the place. Later in the afternoon, she came back again. This time she played a part. I don't know why. Maybe we'll never know why. And she didn't say a word to Fritz. He didn't want her to go home with anybody or to go to a hospital. He knew she didn't need shelter. He tried to fix it up so she could stay here where he could watch to see that she didn't talk and raise a lot of scandal. He wanted to get a doctor and nurse to show that she wasn't really sick or starved."

I said: "We all felt so sorry for her. We drew lots to see who should take care of her. She was a good actress."

"She was on the stage when I met her," said Fritz.

"Well," Marcia continued, "she went home with Miss Rebecca, but in the middle of the night she left and went to Fritz' place. I was there. She found out we were married. She had thought we were only engaged. That made it all the worse."

"Poor Marcia," I said.

Marcia smiled at me as if she were a thousand years old and knew all the sorrows of the world. "The next night she stayed overnight in the store. There was a couch here. She saw it. She got hold of one of the buyers, and made her bring her some food."

"We know about that," said Hank. "But why did she do all this? Can you tell me?"

"Ask Miss Emily," suggested Gaines harshly. "She knows what's in that safe outside the cut-room door."

"I know that," I put in eagerly. "The safe's just there to hold stuff from the store that we don't like to leave out overnight. Stuff we are writing ads about or having pictures taken of."

"It was more than that," insisted Marcia. "There's a small safe inside the large safe. A sort of jewel box set in a panel behind a rack, with a combination and a key. Ask Miss Emily what's in it. It's something to do with the jewelry she had reset for Mrs. Worster when she was in New York. And then Mrs. Worster had to go West when her daughter was killed, so the jewels are still there. Mary knew about the jewels and she wanted them."

"Impossible," said Hank feebly.

But, watching Marcia, I believed she was telling the truth. There must be some reason why Miss Emily made it her business to tend to things in the safe after advertising department hours. Often I've seen her going in as we were leaving. I've often seen her coming out when there didn't seem to be any reason why she should have gone in. But if she was in charge of the resetting of some jewels that belonged to the newly-rich Worsters, that was explained.

"All right," Hank said, "Mary came here to get the jewels. She blackmailed Miss Tates into bringing food for her. Why? You already knew she was here."

"But we didn't," Marcia said. "We didn't until afterwards. Nita told Fritz the second day that somebody had stayed. He was sitting there trying to make up his mind what to do. He was going to Miss Emily to ask her and then all this happened. And I knew by this time that I was going to have a baby. It was everything at once." Marcia paused a moment, then went on:

"Fritz was going to stay here after the place closed that night and tell Mary she could have anything if she'd only go away and let us alone so we could be happy together. He asked me if he could have my ring. He had to tell me what he wanted it for. Of course I was willing to do anything for him. He needn't have been afraid to tell me he'd been married before. A little thing like that wouldn't have turned me against him."

The way she looked at Fritz made me feel shivery. Hank said:

"Did you see her? Did he?"

"No. He stayed for an hour and looked everywhere, but couldn't find her. The next morning we were the first here. The night watchman let us in. I got my model things on first, so that if anybody else came I'd have an excuse for being here early. To see if the things fit or would have to be altered before the fashion showing we were going to have today. Then I went upstairs."

We saw Fritz' arm tighten around Marcia, and she said: "We talked to her. She laughed at us for being in love. Said she'd let us alone if I'd trade my diamond for her amethyst. I hated to put it on after it had been on her hand, but I thought I'd do anything to have her let Fritz alone. So I traded. This amethyst is hers, of course. Not a good one. Worth a few dollars, not more."

Hank asked: "Was she alive when—you left?"

Marcia looked frightened. "When we left, she was still alive. That was a little before eight."

I thought she emphasized "we" a little. Hank probably thought so, too. He asked: "Were you together when you left the office?"

Without blinking, Marcia looked him straight in the face and said: "Yes." But I knew she was lying.

Hank thought so, too. He said: "Gaines saw her alone for a few minutes, after you left?"

Marcia stuck her fingers in her ears. "I won't listen," she cried childishly.

Hank said: "I know the answer. Gaines, was she alive when you left?"

"Yes. At least I—I think so."

Sharply Hank asked: "What do you mean? Don't you know if she was alive? Don't you know if you killed her?"

"I said what I had to say and I turned to go," Gaines explained. "As I walked across the room I heard her gasp, and then I heard her shriek. But I didn't turn around. I knew her tantrums; they only got worse if you paid any attention to her. I walked out of the room and closed the door behind me without looking at her again."

Hank said: "And she might have been killed while you were in the room? Is that possible?"

"Yes. I don't know what I heard. There may have been other sounds. I keep remembering sounds that probably weren't there at all. I'll never lose the memory."

"My poor Fritz," crooned Marcia, comforting him.

"That was about eight?"

"Nearer eight-twenty, I'd say. Almost time for the store to open."

"And later?" asked Hank gently.

"Later I went down to the door to talk to Lane. To let it appear that Marcia had just come in and walked upstairs to change to the Schiaparelli outfit she was talking about."

"And I," said Marcia, "went back to talk to her again. I couldn't get her out of my head. She wanted something so desperately. She seemed so unhappy. After all, I had Fritz and she hadn't. So I thought I might be able to help her. I went back up to the seventh floor. I was too late."

"She was dead?" Hank asked.

"She was dead. The door was standing open. She was lying on the floor with her throat cut. I—God help me—I thought for a minute that Fritz had done it. I knew when he told me he didn't, that he couldn't have. But then, for a minute, I was almost crazy. The blood was still coming out. I got some on my hand and on her ring. I washed my hand, but didn't see what was on the ring. Not then. The shears were lying there. I even picked them up and wiped off the handle, because I was afraid Fritz might have done it and left fingerprints. I wiped off the door-knob, and locked the door from the inside. There's a catch that works that way. I came out through the cut-room. Through this door. I met Nita and came here with her. As if I didn't know what was behind the door."

I didn't even know that Clancy was in the room. My eyes had been on Marcia and Hank and Gaines. But now Hank said: "Get it transcribed, Clancy, and let them see it and sign the statements. I think this ought to help us a lot."

I got up and went out, Hank following me. Marcia was in Gaines' arms and they both seemed to be crying a little. So was I. Hank said gruffly: "You're like all the rest of them. Cry every two minutes. Take my handkerchief."

He thrust the ragged white thing at me and I made a mental note to order him some new linen ones. I rather liked the idea of giving him something.

"Well," he said, "what now? Cigarettes?"

We sat down on some more steps and smoked another cigarette apiece and considered the rest of the evidence. This time we decided that they were telling the truth. All of the truth.

"God knows where we'll find a better pair of murderers," Hank said, "but these two are in the clear. I'll bet you a buck on it."

I didn't take it. I wanted to bet on Marcia and Fritz, too, because it was so swell to see people like that about each other in this matter-of-fact world.

We had finished our cigarettes when they came to tell Hank that Lang had confessed to killing Willing.

Lang was the dress buyer. I didn't believe a word of the confession, and said so before the elevator got us down to the floor where the dresses were.

Because it was Willing who had always hated Lang, and not Lang who had hated Willing. Lang had laughed at Willing, and you don't kill anybody you can laugh at. Nobody does.

ELEVEN

I traveled along down with Hank. Not that he especially wanted me, but I couldn't help it. Besides, who had a
better right? Hadn't Mary Paul been killed right next to
my own typewriter desk, right on the floor of the outer ad
office where I walked every day of my life?

Lang was standing there, head flung back, eyes haunted,
when I saw him. He was saying something to Hank and
Hank was looking at him as if he didn't believe a word of it.

"Hell," said Lang, "what kind of a cop are you? I've
heard they use rubber hose to get a confession, but you
won't even take one if I give it to you. Want it engraved
on a white card and presented on a silver tray?"

Hank just looked at him. Then he turned his back and
walked over and sat down in one of the big upholstered
arm-chairs we use for million-dollar customers in the dress
department. "That's one way of doing it," he said. "Do
you charge extra for engraving? And who ever told you
that you know anything about murder or cops, anyhow?"

Lang said: "Well, I'll be damned," and sat down kind
of hastily in another of the chairs. Hank said to the men
standing around:

"Beat it, all of you. We'll call you if we need you."

They stood around and looked helpless for a minute
and then they shrugged various sets of shoulders, and went
on to the elevator that old Frank was still running.

"Got a cigarette?" Hank asked me, motioning me toward a fragile little gilt chair that I sat down on gingerly. It was probably the first time it had been used for anything more practical than to hold a chiffon dinner dress in a window display.

There didn't seem to be much use in answering.

I hadn't any, and I knew that my case in Hank's pocket was empty. But Lang handed out some and Hank took one, offered one to me and one to Lang, then carefully put the rest of them in his pocket. That's the way he is with cigarettes.

Thoughtfully he asked: "Wanted to get action? Or something else?"

Lang said haughtily: "I don't understand. I tell you I murdered them, and you—"

"I say ha-ha," Hank retorted soberly. "You've got a reason. You didn't murder them and you know you didn't. Maybe you know who did and you want to save him—or her—from the penalty. There's a law against murder in this state, you know."

"Nonsense. I killed her. I killed him. Take me to jail. What more do you want?"

It hadn't been so long since I was in the department kidding with Lang about the new dress and my discount. Something had happened since then to give him that drawn and haggard look. Something that would make him confess to two murders he didn't do, just to save somebody else.

"I don't know what in hell makes me so sure you didn't do it," Hank said. "Maybe I'm crazy, and you did. Maybe I'm just one more punk who doesn't know a murderer when he sees one. But if you killed the guy and the gal, then I'll eat my hat."

Lang took a deep breath and said uneasily: "But why are you hesitating? Why don't you take me while I'm willing?"

"Because you're too damned willing. You killed her, you say? What time did you kill her? What color dress did she have on? What color hair has she? What color eyes has she? What color buttons did she have down the back of her dress?"

He fired the questions at Lang like bullets out of a gun. Lang didn't even blink. He just said: "Cut out the comedy. How the hell do I know? I wasn't making love to the woman. I was killing her."

"Yeah? Why?"

"Well, I killed her. She was blackmailing me. She had some letters."

"When did you kill her?"

"This morning. Before the store opened."

"Did anybody see you?"

"No. I just killed her and locked the door and threw away the key. Then I came down here and got to work on some orders that I wanted for the October Opening." Lang was glib now. He was playing with a pencil, scribbling on a card from his pocket.

"You're not left-handed," said Hank, meaningly.

Lang paled a little. "Meaning that she was killed by somebody left-handed? Well, I'm practically ambidextrous. See?" With his left hand, he scribbled awkwardly on his paper.

"So nice to know these things," Hank said. "You killed her left-handed? How were you standing? How did you get at her?"

"Well, I sort of stood in front of her," said Lang desperately, "and I held the weapon, the shears, behind me in my left hand. When she turned her eyes away I grabbed her and held my hand over her mouth so she wouldn't yell. Then I cut her throat."

"With the scissors held in your left hand? And you standing in front of her with her head turned?"

"Yes."

"All right," said Hank. "Now you'd better tell me the truth, don't you think? Anybody who killed the woman stood behind her and grabbed her head back. Cut her throat with the scissors held in the right hand, from the angle used, the police doctor says. There was blood spattered on the floor in front, and on the papers that were on the floor. Even the ones on the desk. No blood on you, but there was probably none on the killer. There would have been, if he had stood in front of her."

Lang stirred uneasily. Stubbornly he insisted: "I killed her. I killed him, too."

Hank took another cigarette and noticed Lang's eyes studying hungrily the last one in the pack. He handed the pack back and Lang lighted up again, too. They forgot about me.

Angrily Lang said: "All right, all right. I didn't do it then. What the hell do I care? But you're a damned fool not to take the easy way. You'll have plenty of trouble finding a better candidate."

"But why did you say you were the murderer?" asked Hank.

Lang shrugged his shoulders. "Why not? Newspaper notoriety, maybe. I'm a headline hunter. Call it that."

"Herring across a path, maybe. Got a cigarette?" asked Hank. Lang got up and wandered into the fitting-room that he used for an office and came out with a new package of Camels.

"Here," he said. "Keep 'em. I've got the rest of a carton. Maybe a herring," he agreed. "Will it do me any good?"

"Did she do it? Or does it just look like she did?" asked Hank, tearing open the package raggedly, and thrusting a cigarette into his mouth.

Lang gave him a. quick glance and said seriously: "Look here, she didn't. I could swear that she didn't. But—she was there. And when they find it out they'll think she did. Especially when they find out a few other things."

I didn't know who they were talking about. "She" might be anybody. I hadn't ever noticed Lang with anybody around the store, but that didn't mean anything. Look at the way none of us knew that Lane, the store detective, was fixing to marry one of the girls in the store until the week before they invited us to the wedding.

I thought around a little. It couldn't be any of the girls in the advertising department. They were a sort of clubby group, with their own department club and a habit of traveling in bunches. Double or triple dates. Things like that.

But Lang said: "I wonder if you know her. I think I'll tell you. You sound like a reasonable kind of a guy who doesn't go off half-cocked. But I warn you that if you put her on the grill I'll commit murder myself and the victim won't be anybody a hundred miles from here."

Hank scrubbed out his cigarette in one of the fancy crystal ashtrays they put in last month for ladies who smoke while they are buying their trousseaux. "There's nobody around now to take down anything for a statement," he said. "Call it off the record for now, and we'll edit it before you dictate it to a blonde stenographer. Tell me, Lang. One of the models?"

"Hell, no. What would a guy like me do with a dress model? I like mine round enough so you don't scratch yourself on their shoulder blades. These dress models wear sizes 12 and 14. My girl wears a 44. She'll be swell to look at if she puts on a few pounds after we're married. She doesn't fuss with her face and her clothes either, like these floozies I buy dresses for and the models who show 'em, I like a girl who's satisfied with her face as God made it and who'll be satisfied to wear gingham house-dresses in a kitchen."

Hank grinned at me, and took another cigarette. I wondered if he was smoking too much. "Quite an idea," he said. "Natural, too. You look at the Paris models and the Paris lipstick until they get your goat." Abruptly he added: "Who's your girl?"

"Agnes Bailey, the commercial artist in the advertising department."

Now I knew. So Lang was the reason why Agnes had gone around lately with that radiant look on her plump, childish face. That was why she had been wearing those pastel gingham smocks around the store. That was why her new shoes were patent leather with perky little bows on them, and why she had suddenly left off powdering her face, so that her cheeks flushed and paled whenever she heard a masculine footstep around the office.

I hadn't seen Agnes all day. And yesterday she hadn't been at the office. Nor had she the day before? I didn't remember. The last time I'd noticed her was when I gave her those toys to draw just before Mary Paul came into the office and fainted that day.

Hank asked: "She here?"

"No. She's home. In her own room. She—she came and left."

"Where was she when I was asking questions?"

"With the customers. She went home. She said she hadn't been upstairs at all, and your men let her leave. Before the second murder. Before the poisoning or the shooting. But—she *was* upstairs. And she did see—Mary Paul."

"Dead?" Hank's tone was sharp.

"Barely. The blood was still spurting. Agnes got some on her smock and her shoes. And the drawing she had in her hand. And her hand."

"Get hold of her," said Hank quietly. "I want to talk to her."

Lang looked at him a minute, hesitated, then went to the door of the fitting-room next to the one where I had tried on my green-yellow dress. "Come out, Agnes," he said.

Agnes wasn't a favorite of mine. I don't like girls who go stolidly about their jobs, looking like fresh, plump country girls in cotton dresses. But today there was something frightening and at the same time terribly appealing about her. Her usually pink cheeks were a little pale, and there were circles under her blue eyes that made them seem dark and mysterious. For the first time I began to see why a man could fall for a girl like Agnes, plump and healthy and sane, with calmness and serenity and motherliness in her nature. Not that she looked so calm and serene today. But the elements were there.

She held her chin well up and the smile she gave Lang was comforting. She went right over and took his hand and held it. Then she looked at Hank, squared her shoulders and asked:

"Well?"

Hank stood looking at her for a moment. Then he motioned her to a chair before he sat down. She sat on the edge of hers, a little like a buxom servant girl at an interview with some woman who is about to hire her.

"You didn't do it, Agnes?" Hank asked her gently.

"No. Neither did Ken. He's been trying to tell everybody he did, because he was sure you'd think I did it. But you know better, don't you? You know we didn't?"

"Tell me about it," Hank asked.

"I hate that woman," Agnes said fiercely. "I tried to be decent to her and she tried to take Ken away from me. She made a play for him the minute she met him."

"Nonsense, honey," said Lang. "She didn't want me."

"No, she didn't. But she was the kind that takes you whether she wants you or not. She just couldn't resist a good-looking man."

The way Lang looked at Agnes got me. She was probably the first girl he'd ever met who had flattered him by being jealous of him and by suggesting that he was a handsome man whom ladies couldn't resist. I looked at his stubby figure in its cinnamon brown suit and its tan shirt, at the somewhat ridiculous nose and the bald head, and realized that Agnes really did think he was handsome. She wasn't capable of pretense. Not Agnes.

Well, it takes all kinds. I looked at Hank and found him watching me, his nose wrinkled in a grin that made me feel kind of warm and nice. After all, maybe Agnes didn't see Hank the way I was beginning to, either.

"I kept thinking of her," Agnes was saying. "I couldn't get her out of my mind that night after she fainted in the store and went home with Miss Rebecca Allen. So after Ken came we walked over to Miss Rebecca's apartment and went in to see if we could do anything to help."

"She took over some chicken broth she had made, and some new-laid eggs her cousin had brought her from the country, and a glass of her grape jelly," Lang said proudly, beaming at Agnes.

She looked at him, too, and I saw the rich color flood her face. It made you feel a little trembly to see how much she loved him.

"Anyhow," Agnes said, "she was lying down in Miss Rebecca's new negligee and she talked to us. To Ken. She—oh, I hated her. She had that sly way of looking at him—at any man, probably—from under her eyelids. And she wasn't really as pale and haggard as she looked, either. She had on liquid powder and a lot of mascara under her eyes. I saw it when the light was directly on her. I bet she didn't really faint at all, but only put it on, for some reason."

She went on to tell the things she had seen and done that evening, and I kept wondering why Miss Rebecca hadn't said anything about this visit to anybody. Not that there was any reason. Still, it did seem queer.

Hank kept asking detailed questions that I couldn't see much use of. He just kept going over and over the times again. Nothing new developed, so far as I could tell.

Except once, when Agnes said she saw the corner of a little red book peeping out from under the pillow of the *chaise-longue* on which Mary was lying.

Hank asked Agnes questions about herself, too. About how she happened to study commercial art and where she studied and if she had ever known any of the people in the store before she came to work here.

Agnes was surprisingly capable in her job. There was something so spirited and free about her fashion drawings that I could never understand her personal stolidity. But now I saw that the spirit was real and the stolidity wasn't. But it took Ken Lang and a couple of murders to show her up. I rather liked Agnes this way. I knew, of course, that she hadn't anything to do with the murder. Or had she? That sudden fire made me wonder?

Hank asked: "When did you come in this morning?"

She grew pale again. She said: "It was almost time for the store to open. I came right in and put on my smock. I was standing there with a drawing in my hand, next to the table in the ad office. I came to get the big shears to cut the paper at the edge. It was ragged. But the shears weren't there and I remembered Nita and Charlie squabbling about them."

"What's that?" asked Hank sharply, looking at me.

"I couldn't find them the day before," I explained, "and Charlie said he hadn't seen them."

"Anyhow," Agnes said, "I started into the cut-room and was about as far as the door to the outer ad office when I heard voices. A woman was standing in the ad office with the shears in her hands. She was holding them by one blade."

"Did you see the woman?" snapped Hank.

Agnes looked a little frightened. She nodded, then said: "The woman was saying: 'You're mine and she can't have you, if I have to kill both of you. The blade of this shears is sharp enough to kill.'"

"The woman—?"

"Mary Smith. Mary Paul. And she was talking to Mr. Gaines."

TWELVE

Hank looked grim. He said to me: "See if you can find Marcia, will you? And Gaines. And don't tell 'em what Agnes said. I'll talk to 'em here. They'll break me at the office for not getting signed statements, but those can come later. I want to get down to the bottom of this business now. It looks bad for Gaines."

He was asking Agnes more questions when I looked back from the elevator. I unconsciously shuddered a little so that old Frank asked me if I was cold. I said no, but I was. It was the intent look of Hank's that made me feel that way.

Gaines was sitting in the cut-room with his arm around Marcia and I heard him say: "Everything will be all right, darling," as I came in. But he stood up, embarrassed, when I came in and listened to what I had to say. Then, without saying anything more to each other or to me, they went on out to the elevator and I saw them disappear.

I didn't ride down with them. I couldn't. I could just stand there with my fists clenched and tears in my eyes trying to bite back the sobs that clutched at my throat.

Everything was over for them. I hated Hank for telling them that he knew everything. He'd tell them now. Maybe he had started already. Because there just wasn't any other way to look at it. Gaines had killed Mary. Maybe Marcia had known about it, too.

I couldn't blame them at all. I think in the same position I'd have done the same thing. Well, they didn't get away with it and my main emotion right now was sorrow that it had to be Hank who found them out.

I hated him a little, even if I knew he was only tending to his job. I hated Agnes, too, with her plump, sensible face, sitting there on the edge of her chair saying the words that would bring tragedy to Marcia, who was my friend, and Gaines who loved Marcia.

I didn't waste any sympathy on Mary Paul. Women like that are made to be killed. The sooner the better, I tried to believe, remembering the things she had done to everybody who had seen her.

But Willing—I didn't understand about him. And Mr. Bertram. And the poison in the sandwiches.

Somehow I kept thinking that Miss Tates knew more about these things—at least, more about Mr. Willing and the poison sandwiches—than she had told.

Slowly, I went down the steps, emerging into the narrow hall behind the fitting-rooms on the floor where Hank was talking to the four of them. Gaines and Marcia. Lang and Agnes.

It was there, just inside the door, that I came on Miss Tates, with her ear to a crack, listening so hard that she didn't hear me until after I called her by name. Then she sat back on her heels and started to cry. The tears ran down her face, leaving rivulets of unpowdered skin against a background of suntan powder.

"Well," I said, "not that it's any of my business, but what are you doing here?"

She said: "Nita, tell him to stop. You make him stop. He'll listen to you. Marcia doesn't know any more about those murders than the man in the moon. And I do—but I can't tell."

I grabbed her arm and turned her around: "Look, Miss Tates, you march right out there and tell Hank what you know, if you can prove that Marcia hadn't anything to do with it. I'm afraid for her. Miss Tates, she and Gaines are married, and she's going to have a baby, and she just isn't up to all this excitement. She isn't strong enough to stand it. For Marcia's sake, tell what you know."

I told her over again, in two or three ways, pulling all the sob stuff I could and being just as sincere as anybody ever was. Because Marcia was my best friend in the store and she looked so fragile that it made me want to cry every time I looked at her. I felt like a traitor for sending her down to Hank, and felt like twice a traitor for having given him the ring I had found in the dress she wore.

Finally, Miss Tates said: "All right."

She squared her shoulders and went on into the room with me, but I held onto her arm so she shouldn't pull loose and run. I thought then that she was ready to do it. But I didn't know Miss Tates.

Hank looked up at me, but he didn't grin. He looked at Miss Tates a little surprised and then Miss Tates said: "Now I'll say what I've got to say, but you let Marcia go. Will you?"

Marcia murmured something to Miss Tates and put her arm around the older woman. "I'm all right," she said then. "Don't worry about me, dear."

Hank said: "We haven't really begun to talk. Sit down, all of you. Maybe we can get somewhere. If we talk off the record this way, maybe we can get to the bottom of it."

We found seats, all of us, and drew the chairs in a circle. I felt that we ought to have cups of tea to help out the illusion of a party, but nothing so frivolous occurred to the others.

"Now, Agnes, say again what you said just before we called Marcia and Gaines down."

Agnes was sitting on the edge of her chair now and she looked a little wilted. She didn't look straight at anybody but Lang who was looking at her with the same solicitous air with which Gaines was looking at Marcia.

She told the story of how Mary Paul talked to Gaines, and repeated Mary's words as she flourished the sharp shears:

"'You're mine and she can't have you, if I have to kill both of you. The blade of this shears is sharp enough to kill.'"

Gaines said: "I didn't tell you that. I was afraid to. She did say it. I think she still wanted me, but she certainly didn't love me. She never loved me. She was just putting on an act. The way she always did when we were married and she pulled a tantrum to make me give her things she wanted."

Hank said hopelessly: "How in hell can I get the truth out of this business when nobody tells me anything? How do you expect me to find a murderer?"

Marcia said: "But Fritz didn't kill her. He told you so."

"Yeah," Hank said. "He told me so. He told me a dozen other things, too, most of which are lies. Listen, can't you label your lies, mister?"

Gaines said helplessly: "But I didn't. She was alive when I saw her. Then I went out and I don't know what happened. She may have been dead. But only if somebody came in and killed her. She groaned, I thought. But then she always groaned. It was part of her act. God, if I only knew." He put his head down on his arms.

Hank said: "Agnes, what did you see then? Tell me."

"Nothing. I went back into the cut-room and waited. I thought they'd be through in a minute. I hardly recognized Mary Paul. She looked different. Sort of—blazing. Not like she did that other day. I sat down and looked at the picture I had in my hand and—and drew another picture on the back of the paper."

"What?"

"A picture of Mary Paul. The way she looked then—blazing. It's there, in the office." She nodded toward the fitting-room where Lang had his desk.

"Get it, Lang. The blood-stained stuff, too. I want to see them."

We waited until Lang came back and handed the things to Hank. I turned my eyes away from the stiffened blood-stain on the smock, and from the smear on the white Bristol board of the drawing. With careful fingers, Hank turned the drawing so we could see the sketch on the back.

Mary Paul looking blazing—as Agnes had said. She looked tall and fiery. Like a sort of Goddess of Liberty, thinner and more lithe, brandishing a vast pair of shears with a shining blade like a short, sharp sword.

It made me feel queer to see her there, as I had never seen her in life. It made her seem real as she hadn't seemed on the two occasions when I had seen her. When she had been shabby and badly dressed in our office and then again when she had been dignified and quiet in death on the floor of the ad office.

This time she wasn't like an artificial manikin, made of stained wax. She was alive.

I saw the surprised look that Hank turned to Agnes and I knew exactly how he felt. I hadn't known, either, that the placid Agnes could draw like that, with spirit and fire. Maybe she wasn't just one more fat girl from the country who had had a few art lessons and been lucky enough to get a job in an advertising department.

Hank said: "There's a reporter downstairs who ought to see this. You'll be famous by tomorrow, Agnes."

Lang looked prouder, but Agnes seemed fussed a little and didn't say anything.

"Agnes," Hank continued, "when did you go back into the room where Mary Paul was?"

"Not more than ten minutes later," Agnes said.

"And she was dead?"

"She was dead," Agnes hesitated, "or almost dead. I thought I heard her try to say something. I thought her hand fluttered. I thought her eyelids closed and then opened again. The blood was still spurting. Then it sort of flowed. I got some on my drawing and on my smock. On my hands, too, but I scrubbed it off."

"Put on the smock." Hank held it out. I saw Agnes shudder away from it a little, but then she put it on willingly enough and stood holding the drawing the way Hank asked her to, while he did some measuring of some kind.

"But Fritz didn't do it," Marcia whispered earnestly. "Even if it looks like it, he didn't do it. I bet Agnes did it herself. She's just the kind who would. A still-waters kind of girl. Nobody knew she was like this." She nodded toward the drawing. "She could kill. She's the kind who could kill."

Marcia was right, I thought, looking at Agnes. But when I saw her looking at Lang I was bewildered. One minute she seemed to be the kind who would kill. The next minute she was just a placid young country girl in love with this man who obviously adored her. I didn't know what to think.

Then Hank turned on Miss Tates. "You came to tell me about Willing, didn't you?" he asked gently.

But she said no. She looked surprised and startled and her face began to get all wrinkled up like that of a baby who's starting to cry. She seemed to have forgotten about Willing for a while. And now we'd reminded her.

She stopped crying and shook her head: "Not Will. I couldn't have hurt him. I've loved him for years. We were practically married once. Only he had a wife and she wouldn't give him a divorce. So we went away together when I was supposed to be in New York. That's what was in Rebecca Allen's diary. And Mary Smith found it."

"So you killed her?" Hank asked. Not believing it, even when he said it. I could see that.

"No. I tried to, but I didn't succeed. They gave me some stuff in a pet store in New York the last time I was on a buying trip. Somebody told me it would be easier to get it there. I told them I wanted to kill a dog that was too old to live comfortably. My poor Mitzi." She started to cry again.

"But you didn't know about Mary Paul then. You didn't know that she'd come or that she'd steal the diary and confront you with the facts."

"No, I told you I bought the stuff for my poor Mitzi. But the pet hospital where I left her when I was in New York found her dying of old age one day while I was gone and made it easier for her. She was dead when I got home. That's the stuff I had. It was still in my desk here at the store when I made up my mind to kill Mary Paul."

"You put the poison in her sandwiches? What was the poison?"

"I bought sandwiches and coffee for her yesterday. She made me do it. Kept laughing at me. Telling me that no man would look at me for love. That nobody could love anybody like me. But he did love me. I know he did. I just couldn't stand it. She said she'd tell everybody and make me the laughing stock of the store. She said I was just the kind she liked to laugh at. It was—like a sickness. Her cruelty. Somebody had to cure her. To kill her. I tried to kill her. I didn't mean for anybody else to eat the stuff. It was for her. I don't know what the poison was. I'm so glad it didn't really hurt Jake."

She started to walk out of the place, and she almost bumped into Miss Emily and Mr. Bertram, who were getting out of the elevator.

Miss Emily was as efficient and neat as ever. Mr. Bertram wore his sling and bandaged arm like a badge of honor. I had never seen him looking so important as he looked that day.

"We are doing our best to help you solve these murders," said Miss Emily, briskly.

"And attempted murders," added Mr. Bertram, importantly, touching his bandaged arm with the fingers of the other hand, as if to call attention to it.

"Tomorrow the ad should pull business and information," suggested Miss Emily, "but in the meantime, we are at your service. Tell us what to do."

"We have organized," said Mr. Bertram. "There are certain questions of policy, of course, that we prefer to decide for ourselves. The detail work we can leave to the police. Now unless there is something important I should like to talk to the newspaper people who are waiting for me downstairs."

He strutted out of the place and a slightly hysterical silence fell on the rest of us. I was trying to hide the laughter that was about to overcome me. Miss Emily smiled wryly and said:

"This shooting has been a blessing to him. I almost hope we never find out who did it. It's a lifetime occupation for my brother, poor soul."

But Miss Tates was turning on her. She said: "You don't understand Mr. Bertram. He's a wonderful man. Will and I both thought so. Nobody ever understood him but us. I'm going to tell him I'll do everything in my power to help discover the man who shot him. This store would go to rack and ruin without Mr. Bertram."

"Hey, there," Hank called after Miss Tates. "What about that attempted murder? Do you think you're going to get away with it that easy?"

"I won't run away," she said loftily. "If you want to arrest me you'll find me tending to my own business. Which is more than you can say about plenty of others in this store, I'd say." She turned on her heel and went to the elevator while we stood there watching her, with our mouths open, until the elevator took her away.

THIRTEEN

Miss Emily looked around her and took the chair that Hank offered. Then she said brightly: "Have you discovered anything? You must tell me everything. I'm so interested."

As if she were sensibly deciding to make conversation with strangers. Her little gray curls were still as tidy at this hour of the afternoon as they had been in the morning when she had hurried into the murder room before the police got there.

Hank said, lighting another one of Lang's Camels: "You haven't told me what I want to know, Miss Emily. The rest of them have."

Agnes frowned impatiently and sat a little further forward on her chair. She looked very uncomfortable.

"What do you want to know?" Miss Emily inquired coolly. "If I murdered these people and shot at my brother and poisoned Jake? Well, I say I didn't, but you wouldn't expect me to say I did if I had done it. Or would you? I lie rather well." Complacently, she brushed the folds of her black dress with her well-manicured hand and studied the effect of the vivid nail-polish against the dark fabric.

"Yes. You probably lie well," Hank agreed. "But you tell the truth admirably, too, if it's advisable, don't you? Will you please tell me the truth or as much of it as you know? For one thing, why did you go into the office when you had been told that the police had instructed everybody to stay away?"

"I'm not accustomed," said Miss Emily, "to being told what to do. Besides, my brother had told me there was something terribly wrong and I'm accustomed to handling these things for myself."

"I don't understand, Miss Emily. Your brother knew what had happened?"

"My brother knew nothing. He had been told something had happened. Being too helpless to investigate for himself, he came to me. I saw what the office boy had already discovered. Just at that time you came."

"Did you know who the woman was? Did you recognize her?" asked Hank.

"Inasmuch as I handled a little blackmail affair for my brother a few months, ago, it is only natural that I recognized the central figure in the blackmailing."

"You dealt with her alone?" Hank's voice was sharp.

"Yes. She spoke of a man, but I saw no man. My brother mentions that he saw the man and identified his letters. I saw no one except the woman. If you want a description of the man, who is also undoubtedly the murderer, my brother can probably give it."

"Why was your brother shot?"

"So he should not be able to identify the man. Because the blackmailing partner was also the murderer. I wish you would keep a close guard on my brother. I expect another attack on his life."

She spoke as calmly as if she were announcing that she expected a shipment of hairnets, but when Marcia gasped, Miss Emily said impatiently: "I'm not a fool. Neither are you. If a murderer shoots once and misses and his victim still lives with no more injury than a scratch on the arm, then the chances are that he will shoot again. If there is another murder, my brother will be the victim."

Whether she was right or wrong the next hour or two would prove. The day was practically gone. That is, of course, the working day.

The first murder had occurred before nine in the morning; the two attempted murders between that time and one o'clock. The second murder was at two, and all of these conversations and scenes had taken up another hour and a half.

Hank was sitting in his deep chair, as far away from me as if we were on separate planets, almost. I wondered whether he even remembered that he had asked me for a date for tonight and whether the date would mean anything to him, as it undoubtedly would to me. There was something about that man . . .

Hank said: "Just as soon as we leave here, I'll put a police guard on Mr. Bertram. He won't be able to stir without having a policeman on his heels. Will that help?"

"Maybe. But if a man wants murder, he'll have murder," said Miss Emily with a tone of finality that made my ears ring.

"Well," Hank said, "we know something now. Something. Not much. Agnes was in the cut-room. Gaines was at the door of the ad office that leads into the hall. Neither saw anybody else. Yet a murderer was there. Both deny having murdered the woman. What does that get us?"

"There's another door," said Marcia suddenly. "There's the one just beyond the safe."

"Great jumping grasshoppers, a hell of a detective I am," said Hank. "Miss Emily, tell me about the safe."

"You want the combination? Or the contents? One mink coat. One set of silver Coronation plate bought from Silverstein, the jewelers, and used for a Coronation window last May. One—"

Quietly Hank scrubbed out his cigarette on the crystal tray and asked, peering at her: "What about the jewels reset for Mrs. Worster, and held until her return?"

For the first time Miss Emily slumped in her chair. "Are they gone?" she asked quietly. "I should have known better than to handle them. They're worth more than this whole store and all its contents. I consented to have them reset for Mrs. Worster because she liked the designs I made for her, and the commission on the job was enough to finance next year's advertising appropriation or a trip to Europe for a couple of the buyers. I wish I'd never seen the things."

"So far as I know," Hank said, "nobody has touched them. But somebody wanted to. Mary Paul stayed overnight in this store, twice, because she wanted to get the jewels."

"Who told her?" begged Miss Emily, looking her age all of a sudden. "My brother? But he didn't know. He couldn't know. I wouldn't trust him with information like that. He talks too much."

Hank didn't know and said so. Marcia stirred uneasily. Agnes said something under her breath and I could see her fumbling for a pencil on the table. She still wore the blood-stained smock and held the bristol board in her hand. I could see that she wanted to draw Miss Emily, so I hurriedly grabbed a couple of display cards from a table and thrust them at her, blank side up. Without realizing who they came from, she took them and began to draw.

The reason we were so terribly upset was that nobody around the place seemed to have the faintest idea about time. We knew that the first murder had happened before the store opened. Sometime between eight and eight-thirty. But more than that we didn't know. The second murder at two o'clock left us still quite uncertain. You never saw such a bunch of time-blank individuals. We are all so dependent on time-clocks in a store that when we don't punch them, we don't know what time it is at all.

Hank said: "Don't try to get out of the store, any of you. All the doors and windows are guarded and you're likely to get yourself shot. If you think of anything else, come and tell me. Miss Emily, did you shoot your brother?"

Miss Emily, without any indication of shock, shook her head. "If I had shot my brother with intent to murder him," she said, "I'm certain the attempt would have been more successful."

Hank rose and bowed. "I am certain," he said politely, "that you are right, Miss Emily. Will you please let me know about the jewels as soon as you find out?"

Miss Emily hurried to the elevator and the other four followed her. I thought maybe Hank wanted to be alone, but he caught at my arm to keep me from going too.

After the rest had gone, he said, without raising his voice: "Put it on paper, Clancy. Off the record, but I want to study it, anyhow. Got everything?"

And Clancy's voice, from the nearby fitting-room, said: "Okay, Hank. Got everything."

Hank poked Lang's package of cigarettes at me and lit the one I picked as soon as we were alone, sitting in two of the deep arm-chairs.

Hank was as grim as ever. "Nice pickle," he said. "I can say more reasons why Miss Emily might have done it. More than most. She could have done it beautifully. But did she?"

"Of course not. Miss Emily isn't like that."

"Somebody who had a mad on Bertram and his wife killed one and tried to kill the other. Willing saw the murder or the attempt, so he was killed. The poison business was an accident. I'll see that they call it ptomaine, if I have a chance. No use pulling in the old girl, since there aren't any hairpins lost. Jake will probably live on the glory for years, and be none the worse."

"Like Bertram," I suggested.

Hank frowned. "No, Bertram's different. With him, it's as if the shooting gave him a spotlighted position. As if he were the corpse at the funeral, the bride at the wedding, the star at the performance. It all revolves around him. We're just background for him. When we get the murderer, he'll pride himself on the job his underlings have done. That's how it is with Bertram. Damned if I blame his wife much for getting what she could from him and then wanting the first husband back again. But what I don't like is Gaines. There's still more to Gaines. And to the blackmailer who looks like Gaines. That's what we've got to get at next, Nita."

"Why didn't you ask, this time?"

"A guy can't think of everything. Besides, I had Clancy back there. It's dirty, doing them like that, keeping records of what they say without letting 'em know I'm doing it. But I've got to know, Nita. I won't put these statements in my report. I'll get 'em to make others and sign 'em. But I had to find out. You know I've got to find out?"

I thought I did, and said so.

He wasn't very personal through all this and I kept wishing he would be. Maybe I'm not man-crazy or anything, but he looked the way I like a man to look, and even at his grimmest he has something.

All of these mix-ups of the lovey-doveys were pretty bad. If Agnes murdered Mary Paul, what would that do to Lang? Besides, why would Agnes do it, when she had so much happiness ahead of her and so much to live for if she'd just give herself a chance?

If Gaines did it, Marcia would be sunk. He had more reason than anybody else. Yet I couldn't see him sticking a scissors blade in a woman's throat.

And this other business. Willing. It just didn't seem real. It was all out of key. It didn't belong in a department store. It was like one of those fantastic stage scenes in which things seem to get more and more grotesque every minute.

Hank reached over and took my hand. "Coming to a show? Or would you rather dance?" he said.

"I got a new dress," I told him. "I bought it from Mr. Lang this afternoon."

"Red?"

"A sort of green-yellow. Yellow-green. Whatever you call it. It's nice on me."

"I don't call it anything," he said, "but if you like it, that's good enough for me. Look, Nita, if I fail on this thing and they reduce me to pounding a beat, would you still go out with me sometimes?"

"Sure. If you go back to a uniform, may I have one of the shiny buttons?"

"Say," he said, "you can have all the buttons. Was there anything left in the bottle that Charlie brought from the corner? I could guzzle a few, or do you think I'd better turn in my badge and get me a job as traveling salesman and let those who can catch the murderers catch 'em?"

I soothed him and we went on talking for a few minutes until he said: "Golly, I forgot all about putting a guard on Bertram. A swell cop, I am. Let's go tend to him before the murderer does."

"How badly was he shot, Hank?" I asked. "And who did it?"

"I did it. You did it. Anybody did it. How do I know? He wasn't shot badly. Hardly more than a scratch. The bandage and sling are just a concession to his natural dramatic instincts. He's the kind of guy who'd have to take ether to have a hangnail cut."

"Did Tates do it? She could have. She was somewhere near where he was. She had just left the lunch-room and was out in the hall somewhere near him."

"Tates?" Hank seemed startled. "But she's crazy about him. Look how she stood up for him."

"But she isn't really crazy about him. It's Willing she adores—or did. Poor old Willing's dead. I keep forgetting."

The rest of the day was like that. Things weren't smooth, any more than they ever are in department stores. Stores like that always have their undercurrent of rebellion, with salespeople squabbling together but joining forces against buyers. With buyers banding in opposition to the merchandise men. With the advertising and buying departments always in rivalry about what goods sells and what doesn't, and why. With stock-girls and porters having their own feuds.

With the artist kicking because nobody gives her enough room to show what she can do, and the copywriter objecting because nobody's going to read swell copy if the printer sets it in six point light.

Sometimes it didn't even seem strange to think of murder happening here. Why, I've seen a buyer come out of Miss Emily's office mad enough to grab a knife and go after her if anybody gave him half a chance. But nobody had tried to murder Miss Emily—so far. That was the funny part of the whole business.

Miss Emily was far more unpopular than her brother. I adored her myself, because her pungent wit was the kind I liked, although she did have a habit of stopping to tell you what she thought of you, no matter who was present.

But lots of people liked Mr. Bertram. For one thing he had that ingratiating way of smiling at you as if you were the only one he wanted to see at that moment.

He was pompous and ineffectual. Exactly the kind of a man who'd say flattering things in an unctuous manner, and I didn't see why a lot of the ladies liked him. But they did. Still, Bertram had been shot at and Miss Emily had been left free from danger.

At least we thought so then.

But ten minutes later we found that the hunting knife had missed Miss Emily by about two inches.

FOURTEEN

Miss Emily wasn't even pale when she brought us the hunting knife and told us how she had heard it whizzing past her head, and how she had turned quickly, but hadn't seen anybody at all.

"A door down the hall banged," she said, "but I couldn't see which one it was. It might have been the door of my own office for all I know. The only thing I'm sure of is that somebody is out to kill a few people in this store and that probably my brother and I will be next."

She was almost as calm as if she were talking about a new hat. Certainly not half so excited as she had been about the advertisement of the murder sale.

Hank looked at the handle of the knife. It was leather covered and Miss Emily was clutching it tightly in her hand, without a handkerchief to protect it.

He said mildly: "Better put it down. We'll want to test it for fingerprints. We have yours, so we can compare them."

So they'd taken her prints. They hadn't taken mine. But Miss Emily shook her head. "I wiped off the handle with my handkerchief," she said. "They didn't kill me, and maybe they won't if they know I've saved them from discovery."

"Well, I'll be gumfloozled," Hank exclaimed. "Don't you want to help us find the murderer?"

"Not especially. Because, after all, he probably has excellent reasons."

She turned and walked away, after putting the knife down on the table next to Hank. Hank sat down weakly and took up the knife in a clean, ragged handkerchief that he had stuffed into his pocket with my cigarette case.

"The murderer bought them by the gross," he said.

"He didn't buy them at all," I retorted. "We took inventory last month and there were a few knives and guns missing. Nobody said exactly how many, but we've been kidding each other about the stick-up trade. I don't know why I didn't think to tell you before," I finished feebly.

I saw the disgusted look he turned on me when he picked up the telephone and talked to the cop at the switchboard. He turned to me once to ask: "Who's in charge of the sporting goods? They said the buyer was in the East."

"The assistant's away on his wedding trip," I told him, "and the two sales-people there are new. Mr. Willing was sort of in charge. He was buyer for that department before he started to buy for the shoe department." I wondered why I hadn't remembered to tell him that before, or why nobody else had. Anyhow, he hadn't asked us. Which wasn't our fault, was it?

"When were the knives and guns missing? Is there any record to say exactly how many are gone?" He was trying to be patient. I could tell that. It just made me angrier to know that he was right.

"The inventory said two guns and a dozen knives," I said, "but Willing told me last week that he thought somebody miscounted. He said he couldn't tell that there were more than three knives missing."

"Three knives missing and two guns," said Hank with a dangerous-sounding gentleness, "and nobody thought to tell the poor, meddling cops. Even you, Nita, and I thought you were a regular guy. Look here, did you ever see this girl, Mary Paul, before the day she came to the ad department?"

He peered at me suspiciously and I felt my face getting prickly. Probably it was red. I couldn't say.

"I hate you," I yelled at him, and started to cry. He didn't do anything or say anything. I looked up and saw he wasn't even watching me. He was looking at the knife, carefully, as if he were trying to remember every detail.

"One down and two to go," he said. I looked at him blankly. "What I can't see," he pondered, "is why the change of weapon. It isn't logical. If the guy had the hunting knives and the guns, why didn't he stick to one or the other and profit by his practice?"

"Maybe he wanted us to think different people did the murders and attempted murders," I suggested. I knew he wasn't exactly talking to me, because he wasn't paying any attention to me at all.

"One down and two to go," he said again. "One knife killed Willing. One gun shot at Bertram. Somewhere in this store are two guns and two knives. Hidden. Now that we know what to look for, we can find them."

He turned to the phone again and gave directions for a thorough search, asking that various members of the store staff be allotted to help the police search for the weapons.

"You might try to look extra hard in the sports goods," he suggested, with a glance at me.

I interrupted him to explain about the perpetual inventory system that would show exactly how many knives were supposed to be in the department and where to find them.

After he passed on the information and sat down again, he rolled a cigarette for each of us and we sat there quietly for a few minutes.

"One more day of murder," I told him, "and I'll call it quits. Next time I need a job I'll take in floors to scrub."

"You! What business is it of yours?" he hooted. "Take a look-see at Marcia, and Agnes, and poor old Miss Tates."

"Mr. Bertram, too. After all, the girl was his wife, wasn't she?" I didn't really feel sympathetic toward Mr. Bertram, but then I didn't like him, anyhow."

Miss Emily, however, was old and fragile. In spite of the gallant lift of her gray curls and the firmness of her thin mouth, I kept thinking that she was an old woman after all, and the things she had gone through this day would have made a nervous wreck out of almost any woman.

She took trouble in her stride. Clancy trailed her all the way around the store, trying to protect her. Maybe he could. But Miss Emily was a fatalist. She said:

"My brother and I will be the next. Somebody wants us out of the way. All of us."

When Hank asked: "Who's 'us'?" she simply shrugged her shoulders and said:

"Get out your list. Who do you think? Mary and my brother. Willing and Jake. And now me. Somebody wants us out of the way."

It struck me at about that time how isolated we were. Outside the store life was going on as usual.

Here, inside, we were in a state of siege, our thoughts tied up with these ghastly murders. In one way, we seemed to be taking the whole business lightly. In another, I think everybody from the stock-girls on up felt the horror of the whole business.

The only thing that saved us from mass hysteria was the fact that everything seemed so unreal that we simply couldn't believe it even when it was happening.

The men now were searching for the two guns and the two sharp hunting knives.

It made me shiver to see the businesslike way they went about the search and the way that all of them, even Hank, seemed to regard murder as an everyday affair.

I realized that it was an everyday affair to them. That was the way they made their bread and butter, just as I made mine writing copy about smooth glacé gloves and frothy lace negligees.

Hank pulled me into a corner when he saw me getting shaky at the unexpected sight of a spot of blood that had fallen on my notebook when Mary was murdered in the ad office.

He showed me an afternoon newspaper. I'd heard newsboys and I knew that somewhere downstairs were hordes of reporters trying to sift out rumors from facts. From time to time they had talked to Miss Emily and Mr. Gaines, and Mr. Bertram. Maybe to Hank, too, but I hadn't seen them.

"The last edition panned me," Hank said. "And you. I always had it in for Trent, of the *Record*. He hinted that the detective inspector in charge was so busy flirting with a brunette that he hadn't had time to get around to finding the murderer. There was one headline about 'Where was Hank Bemis when they killed Willing and tried to kill two other men?'"

I felt sudden anger almost choke me. It hadn't occurred to me that this attraction that Hank and I had for each other was anything for reporters to telephone back to the home paper about.

Hank said: "I'll kill that guy yet. What right has he got to pull you in on it? He's right, though, I should have been tending to my business. If I had, this wouldn't have happened. Any of it except Mary Paul. That was before I got here this morning. Now beat it, Nita, before they shove me back to pounding a beat on account of you. You ought to know better than to pay any attention to a guy like me, anyhow. Why, I wouldn't know how to handle a murderer if he came right up and handed me a confession printed in gold."

"Maybe not," I said, grinning at his grimness. Trying to make him feel better. I succeeded, too, I think, until Clancy came along with Miss Emily in tow, and said:

"We can't find Mr. Bertram or Miss Tates anywhere. They've left the store."

"Impossible. We've got the burglar alarm system switched on," Hank told him. "Nobody can get in or out without a bell ringing in the detective's room on the ground floor."

"We've looked everywhere," Clancy said desperately. "Miss Emily searched all the women's washrooms and I went in all the men's places. We've had people in and out of every department in the place. We even took a look at the elevator shafts. They've gone."

Hank went away with Clancy without another word and Miss Emily sat down next to me on the display stand and drew a deep breath.

"I—" I began.

"I," she began at the same moment. Both of us stopped and I said: "Go on," rather awkwardly.

She said: "You think you don't care about anybody and then somebody's in danger and you find that you do."

Her neat gray curls bobbed and she plucked at a thread in her skirt with a brightly-polished fingernail.

"My brother's a fool," she said. "I thought I'd be relieved if he were dead. I didn't think I had any affection for him at all. Then this happened. The shot. And I kept remembering the way he looked when he was a baby. My mother let me hold him once. He was about three months old and he had a funny red face and a long white dress on. He grabbed at my finger with his little hand and I thought then I'd always love him. Maybe I do still. I don't know."

I couldn't say anything. There didn't seem to be anything to say. I just put my hand over hers and kept it there until she straightened up and said briskly:

"Well, this isn't finding them. Do you think she killed him, Nita?"

"She? Miss Tates?" I asked stupidly, and she nodded. I didn't think so, and I said so. I couldn't understand how Miss Tates had enough force to get herself mixed up in a murder business this way. She was just a funny old maid with a certain flair for buying the kind of corsets that the public would want to wear next season. If she said the buxom figure was going to be in, the town might as well make up its mind to add a few pounds by eating whipped cream and coffee-cake, because buxom figures *would* be in.

She didn't seem to me to be like a potential murderer. But then I remembered a picture of the latest torch murderer I had seen in Sunday's *Post*. A handsome thing with those soulful movie-star eyes. Well, maybe I didn't know what a murderer looked like, anyhow.

The only person I'd seen in years who looked as a murderer might look was Mary Paul herself, the first person to be murdered.

She was one of these under-handed women. I wouldn't have put anything past her. And I'd just seen her once. Maybe I had just let myself be led on to my opinion by the things I'd heard about her. Certainly I had been as sympathetic as the rest of the bunch. Even if I hadn't tried to take her home with me the way Rebecca Allen did.

And just at that minute Miss Emily said: "Rebecca. Rebecca Allen. She's the one I'm thinking about. She hates Bertram. She wanted to marry him once."

I couldn't believe it. Rebecca didn't look like the kind of a woman who'd make a fool of herself over any man. "She and Tates," Miss Emily said. "I thought one of them would rope him in. They fought about him time and time again. That's how they got so clubby. Being together talking about his beautiful gray hair and his smart clothes. Think of it. Two sensible women like that. Bertram must have something. I can't see how they feel like that about him, but they do."

I didn't see how, either, but I wasn't going to say so.

After all, she still loved him. Chiefly because she remembered the little brother he had once been. I hadn't thought that Miss Emily was the sentimental kind, but she was, all right. And this handsome, pompous, middle-aged gentleman, with his fondness for the spotlight, was somebody you couldn't ignore.

I'd always thought of Mr. Bertram as somebody stupid and ineffectual. But maybe he wasn't. Anybody really like that couldn't have won the love of so many women. Mary Paul. Miss Tates. Even Rebecca Allen, whom I sincerely admired.

It was ten minutes later, after we'd been sitting in silence for a while, that Clancy and Hank came back.

Hank looked pale, as if he'd been drawn through a knothole. He jerked his head toward the elevator.

"First floor, Miss Emily," he said briefly. "They need you. They've found them."

She stood up very stiffly. "Dead?" she asked. Her voice sounded almost indifferent, but I could see her hands tremble against her skirt. "Dead?"

"Miss Tates is dead," he said. "Your brother is still living. Has lost some blood and seems weak, but is perfectly conscious. He says she attacked him and then turned the knife on herself. Said she confessed to all the other attacks."

Miss Emily, without waiting for the elevator, was off, down the steps, with Clancy behind her, protectingly stretching out a hand as if to grab at her elbow. We saw them vanishing around the corner of the stairway.

Hank rang the elevator bell.

"Will Mr. Bertram die?" I asked.

Hank shrugged his shoulders and looked grimmer than ever. "The police doctor is on his way back," he said. "Bertram may not be entirely conscious. He isn't sure of anything. He admits that he had a blow on his head, that came from somewhere. And there's a queer, unexplained blow on Tates' head too."

FIFTEEN

This time the newspaper reporters were out in full force. There were six of them right in the department where they'd found Miss Tates and Mr. Bertram. And there was a long, lanky blonde boy with a tiny camera on top of a tall tripod. He was moving the thing about and getting snaps of things all around, including the crumpled body of Miss Tates, and the figure of Bertram, lying there flat on the floor with his feet on an empty carton. Mr. Bertram looked funny until you saw the smear of blood across his cheek, and the smear across his temple. His eyes were closed and he looked a little purple under the bright lights.

Miss Emily was sitting cross-legged on the floor beside her brother, looking down at him, as if she were waiting for him to open his eyes. The policemen and plain-clothes men were milling around the store, systematically hunting for clues.

The camera-toter snapped a quick one of Miss Emily staring down at her tightly clasped hands. I wanted to grab the little trouble-shooter off the tripod and slam it onto the floor. Somehow Miss Emily looked so old and so defenseless there.

Hank motioned me out of the way and then cleared out himself. He beckoned the newspaper men out into the first floor display-room and shut the door on them, leaving Clancy to tell them the things he wanted them to know.

The camera-man rebelled a little, and I heard Hank tell him to stick around if he wanted a good punch in the nose. He followed the rest of them into the room and before he closed the door I saw Hank hand Clancy the key.

Then Hank told one of the other guys to clear the department. I went along with Miss Emily when they herded her with the others into the jewelry department.

It was harder and harder to keep things straight. This last killing didn't seem to explain anything.

Hank had asked questions, but Bertram didn't know much. He said that Tates had shrieked at him and had tried to jab at him with the knife. He had pretended to be worse hit than he was, so she wouldn't stab him again. They must have had a free-for-all in the department. They'd broken one case and slivers of glass lay mixed up with a couple of lace brassieres, and a rather odd-looking satin corset had a jab from the glass and a streak of blood on it.

One display stand had a streak of blood on it, too, as if somebody had smashed it alongside somebody's head.

One dark corner behind a counter was all cluttered up with paper and packing boxes, as if somebody had been hiding there behind the goods that Miss Tates had been unpacking. I wondered whether Tates and Bertram could have been hiding there when Clancy was hunting for them. That little corner was pretty well hidden from the department in general. That's why it was sometimes used for unpacking things, although the stock-room and shipping-rooms were the only places in the store where merchandise was supposed to be unpacked.

Hank was questioning the buyers and the others, one at a time, taking them out of the jewelry department into the corridor. I saw somebody—not Clancy—following him with a stenographer's notebook and pencils.

It was getting late. Time for the store to close under normal conditions and nobody had thought to switch on the lights except in the darker places where they had lights on almost all day anyhow.

I could hear a couple of newsboys calling extras outside and wondered whether all the extras that day were about our store. For all I knew, they might have started another war in Europe.

In the room where the newspaper men and Clancy were talking and asking questions, somebody laughed heartily, and then I could hear somebody pounding on a table or something, as if trying to get attention.

Miss Emily was talking to Hank somewhere. Agnes and Lang were talking confidentially and she was still holding the display card on which she had drawn the picture of Miss Emily. It seemed to be important to her and I wondered if she had been showing it to the reporters and if any of them had offered to use it in their papers.

I didn't dare think who the murderer might be. If Mr. Bertram hadn't himself been shot at and later knifed, I might have suspected that he was the murderer. Chiefly because I didn't like him very much. But I knew I didn't have a chance in picking the right one when I picked him. I had considered Miss Tates a pretty likely candidate, and now she was dead, with a verbal confession behind her saying that she had done all the murders. I don't know why Hank didn't believe that, but I knew somehow that he didn't.

Oh, he believed Bertram's statement. What he didn't believe was that Miss Tates had told the truth to Bertram and that she had used the knife on herself.

Certainly she had stabbed Bertram and then turned the knife toward her own breast. But the way she had done it, hysterically, incredibly, didn't seem to be true, somehow.

After a few words to Clancy Hank called me and drew me into the little alcove where we kept the French hats.

"Buy me a rattle, Nita," he begged. "Or a dunce-cap, or something. I'm nuts. Any cop with sense would accept a death-bed confession like the one Tates handed me. And I don't accept it. I think she was lying. God knows what she expected to get out of Bertram with her tantrums. But she did lie. I can tell a lie a mile off, but some of 'em hit you in the face. This was one like that."

"Did she stab him? Is he dead now?"

"She stabbed him all right. Her fingerprints are on the handle of the dagger that cut him. Her fingerprints are on the other one, too. The one she used on herself."

"The other one?"

"Exactly. The other one." He sounded grimmer than ever. "That's why I doubt that she did the job. Look here. There is something more than anybody could tell us. Bertram is with her. She is crying. About how much she loves him and how much she hates everybody that has ever come between them.

"First she says she could kill anybody who comes between them. Then he felt a little flattered, he says. He asked her, 'Would you really kill anybody? Did you kill— her? My wife? And Willing? The man who loved you?'

"She flashes a couple of knives out of a corset box, he says, and waves them at him recklessly. Tells him she has killed those other people and if he doesn't love her she doesn't want to live either. But she won't let anybody else have him. She flashes a dagger at him and it catches him on the face. He closes his eyes, and remembers feeling something hot on his face. Then something bumped at him, he says, and he went out like a match. Fainted."

"From the knife-wound?"

Hank shook his head. "Probably not. There's a funny kind of bump on his temple. Probably something hard hit him. The display stand we found, or something else. And there's a bump on the woman, besides the knife-wound that probably killed her."

"Did she kill herself?"

Hank shrugged his shoulders. "How do I know? She's dead, after announcing she killed these people and intends to kill him and herself. Then she lunges at him with the knife, but doesn't hurt him much. Just a scratch. Not much worse than a hangnail so far as any permanent damage is concerned. If she wanted to kill him and then kill herself, she didn't do such a good job. Surely after all the practice she's had today, she ought to do better than that."

Hank was fumbling for a cigarette. I saw Charles in the next aisle and beckoned him. "There's a carton of cigarettes in the bottom drawer of my desk," I told him. "See if you can get 'em before somebody else accomplishes a murder somewhere around the place."

He was back in a hurry and he gave the cigarettes to Hank instead of to me. He knew Hank by this time.

We didn't say anything much while we were waiting. After Hank was drawing on a cigarette he said: "Suppose Miss Tates didn't? What then? Who is capable of coming in after she has made a stab at Bertram and a stab at herself? Who could have done the job thoroughly when she was just making a bluff? Bertram says he turned his head away and closed his eyes and pretended to be unconscious. Says he couldn't get the knife away from her, so he thought he'd pull a stunt like that. Says anybody else might have come and he wouldn't know?'

"Bertram isn't stupid enough not to know when somebody is bashing him on the head," I said. "Or is he? If he closed his eyes, so Tates would think she had killed him."

"She wouldn't know whether people closed their eyes when they were killed with a blade," Hank was rubbing out his cigarette and lighting another, "but if she had killed Mary Paul and Willing, she'd know from experience. Therefore, if she killed them, she'd know that he wasn't dead. She was lying to Bertram, and we've got to go on looking for a more likely murderer."

We were left at that, when five-thirty came. They let us go home, after all sorts of preliminaries, and I saw Hank standing at the door looking after Mr. Bertram, who was limping toward a taxi with Miss Rebecca on one side and Miss Emily on the other. Mr. Bertram seemed to be enjoying himself a lot.

Hank grabbed my arm as I started to leave and said: "432 Oak Street? Seven-thirty? Wear that new dress you bought. Red, wasn't it?"

I nodded, then shook my head, and went on down the street with the dress box under my arm. Lane was checking us out, as usual, and he said seriously:

"Look here, Miss Nita, we oughtn't to go home until we get this whole business straightened out. The police ought to have more sense. Once let the murderer get away and how do you know whether you'll get him back? You tell your boy friend he ought to stick to business."

I said: "You can't expect a man to work more than ten or twelve hours a day at the most, Lane, and most of them only work eight. Surely a policeman's got a right to take out a girl-friend after his day's work. Didn't you elope with Bessie right in the middle of that shop-lifting business?"

"I didn't elope with Bessie. We told you about it and all of you came to the wedding. I was back on the job the next day and we didn't take any honeymoon till I found the shop-lifters. Remember?"

"Well, Hank'll be back on the job tomorrow, too, and he'll find the murderer if there's one to find."

I swung down the street feeling that Lane was probably right and wondering whether Hank shouldn't have done more than he did. Maybe talking to me had held him up some. Certainly the murders and attempted murders while he was there hadn't helped his reputation any.

I soaked in the tub with my best bath-salts and dabbed some of that Parisian perfume behind my ears and on my hair. The yellow-green dress was as becoming as I knew it would be, and Hank and I had one of those unforgettable evenings when you keep thinking to yourself: "This is important. I'll remember this."

He didn't kiss me at all, until after we had danced a little and were back on my front doorstep. He said: "Next time we'll have dinner at that little place on the roof. Remember the one I told you about? We can see the stars from there. And the moon."

"I've had a lot of moon tonight," I said, unsteadily. I didn't mean the highball we'd had after the dance or the cocktail at dinner, either. The way that man made me feel when he looked at me was plenty disturbing.

He kissed me rather lightly, finally, and said: "Tomorrow will be hard, Nita. I haven't talked much about it. But if I lose my job because they think I've spent my time with you instead of tending to business, what then?"

"The woman always pays," I said.

He didn't laugh. "This time you're right," he said. "Mary Smith paid. And Miss Tates—she didn't do those murders, Nita. She couldn't. Oh, she scratched Bertram with the dagger, but she didn't do much damage and she didn't have sense enough to know that he was shamming when he closed his eyes. I guess he's telling the truth. She probably confessed to the murders when she saw that he'd think a hell of a lot more of her if he thought she'd commit murder to get him. But she lied. And when his eyes were closed somebody biffed him. When he went out like a light, they biffed her too. Then when she was out, they killed her. They took a chance that he might wake up and see. But he didn't."

"Sounds logical. But who is 'they'?"

He shrugged his shoulders. "Anybody. Emily—maybe. She'd have more nerve than anybody in the place. Or Lang and Agnes, working in a team to be quicker. Or Gaines and Marcia working the same way. Or Jake, the photographer. Think of Jake?"

Nobody ever thought about Jake, except when he did something wrong and we got at him for it. That's what a photographer is when you use him for commercial stuff and don't let him go temperamental on you.

"But Jake was one of the victims," Hank went on. "Besides, what did he have on any of the people murdered? He didn't know Mary Smith. He hadn't ever talked with Willing, except on business. He hadn't any quarrel with Bertram or Miss Emily. Miss Tates had never done anything to him."

"No? Well, what about the poison? Tates says she put it in the food for Mary Smith. But Jake ate the stuff and he could have died. He owed her something for that," I said, looking up at the moon and wondering what all this talk had to do with a man and a girl under the moon.

"It all comes back to Miss Emily, then," he said. "Or Gaines with Marcia. Or Lang with Agnes. All of them knew how to get hold of the weapons. Anybody could have used them, sharp as they were."

"But somebody threw a hunting dagger at Miss Emily," I said stupidly.

He looked down at me and grinned. Gently, as you talk to a child, he said: "Maybe she was lying, too. How the hell do you know, brat?"

Then he kissed me again, lightly, and I went on in and left him standing on the doorstep.

SIXTEEN

They counted the customers that came into the store the next morning and wouldn't let more than a certain number in each door at any one time. So the place wouldn't be stampeded, I guess. Just the same, you never saw anything like it in your life. Before noon we had sold out all the stuff we'd bought for the whole week of September Sales, and were rummaging in the stock-rooms for all the lemons the buyers had brought in for years. Nobody kicked at the prices or the goods. They bought like crazy and they went out beaming, after stuffing their clues with their names and addresses and sales-checks into the boxes along the west corridor.

If those clues had all been real clues we'd have been sitting pretty. We got somebody from the police department and somebody from the business bureau to comb through the customers' clues and we came out finally with three things that might have been clues and probably weren't. By that time the murders were solved, anyhow, and business was still grand, so that we could easily afford to hand out the ten prizes, even if we didn't get anywhere with the clues. That helped Miss Emily keep on the right side of the Better Business Bureau, anyhow. For a little while nobody was so keen on the notion of letting her get away with her sale ideas. But that's a different story.

Hank was too busy to look at me and that was just as well, because I was too busy to look at him. Miss Emily and Mr. Bertram were everywhere. For the first time I saw Miss Emily with her smooth gray curls rumpled and Mr. Bertram looking pathetic and rather touchingly busy instead of just pompous and ineffectual. He was different somehow and I kept wondering if it had been Miss Tates' death that had done things to him.

Nobody had got Tates straight yet. Hank had probably settled it in his mind that she had confessed to the murders in an attempt to make Bertram think her more fiery than she was. But he was willing to swear that she hadn't really done them. She was responsible for the slight knife-wound that Bertram had, but not for the blow on his head. And she certainly hadn't committed suicide by bruising herself with something heavy to stun herself and then cutting her own throat afterwards.

No, that would have been too much.

There were policemen all over the store. I had a hunch that Miss Emily had hired enough private detectives to put on a good minstrel show, because who else would all of these neatly dressed men be? They certainly didn't buy things, although from time to time one of them would fight his way to a counter and price something without buying it. I could see the sales-girls ready to scream with nervousness before the morning was over. But it wasn't so bad, after all, because they made a nice bonus on everything over their quota of sales.

We missed Willing and Miss Tates terribly, but the shoe assistant was a nice young chap with executive ability and he was wading into his new duties with an interest that promised well for his new contract after this business was over.

Miss Rebecca, from the advertising department, had gone on down to the corset department and was handling all the details of Miss Tates' job. After all, they'd been friends for years and had probably talked shop from time to time.

We didn't have much to do upstairs but, as I had expected, Miss Emily decided that we'd better stick around in the store where we were most needed.

I sold $10.95 dresses for Mr. Lang for awhile, then Agnes came in and I gave up my job to her and went in search of Hank.

He was sitting in the cut-room on a tall stool with a bunch of index cards in front of him and I thought he looked kind of worried. As soon as he looked up I went and took another package of cigarettes out of the almost empty carton and put it in his hand. He puffed gratefully at me before he spoke. "Listen, kid, what do you know about Miss Rebecca? Are you sure she didn't know who Mary was when she took her home? And are you sure that Mary didn't run away because she was afraid of Miss Rebecca?"

That was a new one on me and I said so. "Miss Rebecca has worked here for years. Been everything in the store. She ran an elevator once. She's forty-five, maybe. She and Tates were always together, and I think Miss Emily knew her when she was a kid. What else do you want to know?"

"She and Tates were in love with Bertram. Yet both she and Tates were interested in Willing. How do those things jell?"

"They might have been man-crazy. Old maids are, sometimes." But I didn't think these two were, even when I said it. Especially sane Miss Rebecca, with her sharp wit and her kind heart.

Hank shook his head. "No, I can't even think that Miss Rebecca ever liked Bertram, in spite of what Miss Emily says. She's got more sense than to love that nincompoop."

I thought so, too, and said so. Then I remembered how solicitously Miss Rebecca had helped Mr. Bertram to his taxi last night, and I wondered. After all, strong women have loved weak men before this.

I explained to Hank how I felt about it and left him, still studying his index cards, while I went to Miss Emily's office. To my surprise, she was there.

Spread on the desk in front of her were some jewelry boxes. One of them was open and I caught sight of a pair of clips that were rhinestones, I thought, until Miss Emily held the box to me and said briefly:

"Put them on, if you want to, for a minute. Just to say that you've worn the Reinstrom brooch."

I fumbled with the things and almost dropped them. Miss Emily showed me how the pair of clips screwed together to make a brooch and how they came apart again for dress clips. I refused to put them on, though.

Real jewels make me uncomfortable. I never even wanted a diamond ring. There's something so frightening about so much value tied up in something that is absolutely of no real use in the world. Maybe you wouldn't feel that way, but I do.

Hank understood, too, because later he gave me a typewriter and called it my engagement ring.

I shuddered a little when I gave the jewels back. Miss Emily shoved all the boxes into her top desk drawer and locked it. She put the key on a gold chain around her neck, and said: "I guess they're as safe here as anywhere. If that Worster woman isn't back this afternoon I'm taking them to the bank. I should have done it before this."

After a little silence, Miss Emily stood up and said: "Rebecca didn't do it, did she, Nita? She loved Tates. I know she did. And Willing loved Tates, in spite of the way he acted in public. I've heard him talk to her when nobody knew I was there. You'd have been astounded."

I thought of pudgy Mr. Willing and of fat Miss Tates poured into her dark satin dresses with their crisp white collars and cuffs and somehow I wanted to cry. Miss Emily patted my hand and nodded. "You see, too," she said. "Look, Nita, if I'm the next, I want you to carry on."

"Me?"

"Yes. Nita, in my will, I've left you the controlling interest in the store. Keep it running if it isn't too much of a job for you. I—I hope to have a chance to work out something so you can have an income from it without doing the work yourself. But if I go too quickly to change my will, you'll have it and do your best, I know."

We shook hands on it and just then the door into Mr. Bertram's office opened and he came in, importantly, with some papers in his hand. I wondered if he had heard what we were talking about. I couldn't remember if the door to his office had been closed or open. He didn't say anything about it, anyhow.

He said: "Spare me a minute, Em?" in that brisk tone he put on when he felt important, so I left them together.

I looked down at the crowd on the first floor from the mezzanine balcony where the accessories were sold, and everybody looked more than a little crazy. The advertising department wasn't working at its job, because nobody knew whether there'd be anything left to sell. I sat down on the steps in a corner of the mezzanine, away from everybody. Nobody used those steps much, since we had the elevators and the escalators, so it was the only quiet corner I'd found yet. I took my little notebook out of my purse, and a pencil, and started to map out a full-page follow-up ad for Tuesday, if we had enough stock in the house to keep open that long.

Pretty soon I heard somebody coming and looked up to see Miss Emily and Mr. Bertram standing at the railing on the balcony. I started to go to them, but I wasn't quite there when I heard Bertram say:

"Surely, Em, you wouldn't want me to be afraid."

His sling was around his neck, but he had taken his arm out of it and the black silk handkerchief swung loose. Miss Emily took hold of it and swung him around a little. I couldn't see her face when she said:

"Don't be a fool, Bertram. Take care of yourself. To the rest of them you're just an old fool. But—you're still my kid brother to me."

To my surprise, I saw Bertram slip an arm around Miss Emily. He said: "They won't kill you, Em. I won't let them. And I'm perfectly safe. They tried to get me twice, but they didn't."

Emily asked: "Bertram, Tates didn't do that to you, did she?"

"Damned if I know. She said she did the rest. I know she poisoned Jake, but she didn't mean to. I knew she had the stuff. She didn't tell me at the time. But I—don't know."

"She did—cut you? The way you said?"

"She cut me. I shut my eyes, so she'd think I was helpless and wouldn't hurt me any more. Em, listen." He stopped for a moment and his voice was strange afterwards, as if he were remembering something that hurt more than a little. "Once before she cut me, with that little steel paper knife I used to have on my desk. Ten years ago."

"Not the time you said there were burglars and called the police?"

"Yes. That time. I couldn't give her away. She said she'd never do anything like that again. And I know she only did it because she was jealous. She said I liked Rebecca better than I did her. At the time I did. But after she hurt me— then it was different. Things were wonderful then, for a little while. We almost got married then."

Miss Emily turned around then and caught my eye. She took her hand away from her brother and said sharply:

"What about Tuesday's ad, Nita? Anybody think about that?"

I held out the notebook in which I had penciled a few lines and went swiftly into an explanation of the high points.

Miss Emily nodded. "Give me the book. I'll see if any changes are needed. You'd better go to the jewelry department and help out a while. They've got more customers than they'll be able to take care of in a month of Sundays."

I went. We all did what Miss Emily wanted us to do. If she had asked the advertising manager to polish the shoes in the display case of the shoe department I'm sure he'd have done it without a word of protest. She had us trained, I guess.

The counter was piled high with jewelry boxes and displays. You'd have thought that you were in a store where real diamonds were being offered for $3.98.

I waited on six women at once without getting my breath and then went on to another six. It kept up that way, with us fighting our way through the litter of boxes and tissue paper behind the counter in an effort to get a turquoise bead necklace wrapped up before the customer decided she'd rather have a jade bracelet.

One woman insisted that she had to have rhinestone clips and there weren't any rhinestone clips. I burrowed under the mess of boxes, vaguely trying to find some where I knew none were. One of the girls said over her shoulder: "I just saw some rhinestone clips in a box there in the second drawer, under some other boxes, when I was looking for a pearl clip. A white box that looks like satin. There isn't any price on them, but they look good. Maybe they're the five-dollar bunch that the buyer ordered for next week. You'd better ask her."

I got into the corner and browsed until I found the box with the clips. I opened it and all I could think of was a silly catch phrase from a silly story:

"Honey," the old mammy was saying, "is dem real rhinestones?"

Because these clips were more than real rhinestones. They were real diamonds. They were the diamond clips that Miss Emily had shown me this morning. And here they were, all mixed up with junk jewelry.

I got out of there with the clips in my hand and went to look for Miss Emily. Then after I found her and got her started on her way down to the jewelry department to identify anything else that might be there, I took the key she gave me and went to her office with Hank.

The door was closed, but we could see that the lock had been forced. All of the jewelry was gone.

Hank looked at me and I looked at Hank. "Three murders," he said. "Three more attempts at murder. No, four, counting Miss Emily. An attempted robbery, which probably worked, if this is all that's left out of the loot. All in less than two days."

"We do pretty well in our store." I made for the jewelry department, followed by Hank.

Efficient Miss Emily had had the department roped off and some policemen were keeping the crowd away from that part of the store. The rest of the departments seemed to be having business as usual, but Miss Emily had all the jewelry sales-girls and the buyer rooting through the paper and boxes and junk jewelry to find the Worster jewels.

Miss Emily had found the most important piece on the floor under some crumpled tissue paper. When we came she managed to unearth more, carefully hidden in places where nobody would bother to look at them and where it would be very simple for anybody to come along and grab them. Or even to buy them.

Think of picking up a diamond necklace from the place on the floor where you had hidden it and saying: "I want this necklace from the $4.95 counter. I'll just put it in my bag. You're in a hurry, so I won't wait for it to be wrapped."

Hank picked up a ruby pin that I wouldn't have worn to a dog fight. It was about the ugliest and most expensive thing of its kind I'd ever seen. But I went away and let the rest of them look, because I didn't know enough about jewelry to differentiate between a beer-glass pendant and a diamond set in platinum. That's just the way I happen to be.

And that is how I happened to come on Mr. Bertram sitting in his office, crying, with his head bent on his desk.

SEVENTEEN

He didn't even raise his head when I went into his office. He just sobbed heartbreakingly. I started to tiptoe out of the place, but he must have heard me because he raised his head and looked. I saw his face sort of tighten and get smooth and plump again instead of loose and vague.

He said, with a certain dignity: "I didn't mean for Miss Tates to die."

"Then you don't think she was responsible for what happened?" I asked stupidly.

"No. Oh, she cut me, but if I hadn't been hit on the head just then, things would have been different."

"Did she kill herself?"

"No, I thought she did, first. Now I know she didn't."

"How do you know?" I felt like Hank, asking questions. Mr. Bertram took it very calmly.

"Whoever hit me, hit her. She had already cut me. Then the person who hit her stabbed her. Killed her. I'm sorry she had to die."

"But why did Miss Tates have to die? Why would anybody want to kill her?" I had to get somewhere and yet I didn't know what questions to ask.

I kept thinking of Hank and wishing he'd come. I kept thinking that maybe Tates had told Bertram something that might be a clue—if I could only label it as such.

153

"She saw one of the murders," Bertram said. "That's why she had to die."

"How do you know? Did she tell you, Mr. Bertram?"

He nodded. "She told me she saw somebody kill Mary Smith. But she didn't blame the person. She said she had tried to kill Mary, too, but had failed and had only hurt Jake instead."

"Did she tell you who did it?"

"No. I think she thought I knew already. She seemed to think—" He stopped and cleared his throat. His eyes were still blurred from his crying, and his voice was husky.

"Who?" I almost whispered it.

But he shook his head. "That's what I asked. She just looked at me kind of strangely then. And when I asked again she held up her head and told me she did everything herself, for love of me. That she was going to confess. Then she said no. She'd kill herself. But she'd kill me first. That was when she cut me and I closed my eyes. Then something hit me and I didn't know anything else until everybody came, and she was dead."

There was a kind of dignified simplicity about his tale. Now he seemed more likeable than he had ever seemed before and I felt my heart go out to him in sympathy until I realized that he was the same self-centered, pompous ass that he'd always been and that he was putting on an act even then.

I hated him for a minute, and wished he had been the one to die instead of this woman who had certainly loved him.

But I'd had my lesson about thinking of persons who could better be spared than the ones who had been murdered. When I'd talked about Willing, for instance, and had come on him afterwards with the knife in his back and that terrible leer on his face.

After all, what did I really know about this man? Only that he seemed, on the surface at least, to be an ineffectual, pompous individual, with a sense of his own importance, especially since he had considered himself the target of a murderer's venom.

Still he must have more than that to him. One woman had been willing to marry him. Two others were in love with him and would have been willing to marry him if he had proposed at any time in the last ten years. Women don't fall for nincompoops. Or do they? I wouldn't know. I don't know much about women, anyhow. Except the way they like you to describe the aluminum saucepans and rayon dress goods to make 'em want to buy in a department store.

I went on out pretty soon and left Bertram to his tears. He was certainly entitled to them after what he'd gone through in the past couple of days.

A bridegroom a week ago, after a courtship during the first marriage of the bride, followed by a blackmail plot in which the bride was mixed up in some way. Then the murder of his wife. If that wasn't enough, he got shot himself and, later, stabbed. Both trifling wounds, but the shock must have been plenty. Then the woman who loved him confessed to the murders. I didn't believe her. I'd heard too much about old maids in love who confess to things they never do in order to get a higher standing in the eyes of the beloved.

You never saw a store like that store of ours on that day. The elevators were jammed. The salesgirls were in frenzies. The sales-books were being filled up and okayed and stacked ready for checking. We'd called on all the Christmas extra girls to come in and help sell, and all the models were down on the first floor selling—or rather taking orders. Nothing needed selling. People were buying like crazy. Taking things home with them, too, instead of ordering stuff to be sent. It was just as well. I could see our delivery service being stalled—"paralyzed" was the word the newspapers would use later—because no day's business, even at Christmas, had ever called on so many store facilities.

It was a day, all right. There was something a little insane about the atmosphere. Yet it wasn't ghastly or anything like that. There wasn't anything ghoulish about the way the people hunted for clues and put them in the clue boxes. It was as if they were in some cheerful kind of game where everybody was a gay winner or a gay loser and where it was a lot of fun to do the actual playing. I didn't feel right about it and I knew none of the regulars did.

After all, the murderer might be loose in the store somewhere. How did we know? But you can't shut up a store indefinitely, and Hank and the police had talked to everybody and hadn't gotten anywhere. They didn't have enough evidence to hold anybody, and so far as I could tell they didn't even know who had had a fair chance of being the murderer.

We'd had two confessions so far. Ken Lang, the dress buyer. We knew he wasn't the one, but he had only confessed because he thought we'd accuse Agnes. And Tates.

If all else failed, we could accept Tates at her own valuation and let her be the goat. But nobody could prove anything.

That was where we were by noon of the second day. I met Hank in the employees' lunch-room, where I went to grab a cup of coffee and some food of some sort.

He got me a plate of spaghetti and some watery canned corn. We poured some bluish cream in our coffee and settled down at the corner table.

Hank looked worried. "I'm scared to be with you, Nita, because if anything else happens while I'm here, it'll be your fault and mine."

I knew what he meant. I'd caught sight of a newspaper in Mr. Bertram's office. The headlines had roared about us flirting on the stairways while murder was being done. One paper said something about catching murderers being a little more a detective's business than making love to copywriters.

"Have you got anywhere?" I didn't look at Hank while I talked. I could see Jake, the store photographer, looking eagerly at us from the other side of the room and I had a hunch that one of the reporters had probably got at him with promises of newspaper jobs if he turned in anything on the murder. From what I knew of my news pals, that was likely.

"Clancy thinks it was Tates." Hank's voice sounded indifferent, but I knew better.

"It wasn't?"

"I don't see how it could be." Hank fumbled for a cigarette, but I pointed at the No Smoking sign. He sighed and took up his cup of coffee.

"Neither do I. But we'll have to let it go at that and build up as good a story as we can, I guess, if we don't want to be panned too much. What the hell. This isn't the first set of murders where the police took the handiest murderer because the newspapers hounded them into it."

"Who did it, Hank?"

Hank looked across the room at Jake's leering face. "There's the guy I wish it was," he said. "But it isn't. If that sap snaps a candid camera shot and hands it to the *News* reporter the way he did this morning, I'll kill him myself and call it a good job."

"I didn't see the *News*. When did he take your picture?"

"When did he take *our* picture, you mean. Yours, too."

I took one look at the picture he reluctantly drew from his pocket and took a gulp of my coffee. I needed it. Hank fumbled again for a cigarette and then stopped when he saw the sign. But this time I reached over and took the crumpled package out of his pocket and put it in his hand.

"You'd better smoke two at once," I said. "I can't afford to get fired this week for smoking on this floor."

The picture showed Hank and me beaming fatuously at each other. Hank seemed to be holding my hand and to be about to kiss me. Maybe it was faked. Maybe it wasn't. But there was something rather hauntingly familiar about the expression on Hank's pictured face, and I could remember at least half a dozen times the day before when he'd caught at my hand and looked as if he were about to kiss me. Well, what difference did it make?

Hank put the picture back into his pocket rather carefully. Maybe he didn't hate the idea as much as he seemed to.

Miss Emily came into the lunch-room and stood at the first table, looking around. Hank rose and placed a chair for her beside us. She sat down, saying:

"I'd like some coffee, please." When Hank went to get it, she grabbed at my hand and said:

"Nita, Bertram told Mary Smith about those jewels. That's where she got it. And she probably told Gaines. I'm sorry for Marcia Ames, but I think Fritz Gaines is tied up with this business somehow."

"Oh, no!" I kept remembering Marcia's face as she put her arms comfortingly around Gaines when he had gone all to pieces the day before.

"Nita, did Bertram tell you that the blackmailing man looked like Gaines?"

"Yes, Miss Emily. I don't think Hank believed him. Maybe Hank thought he was just trying to be important or something. Did you see the man, too, Miss Emily?"

"No, but Bertram was telling the truth, Nita. He would lie to make himself more important, but not to make Gaines more important. You see?"

I saw. Hank came back with the coffee then. A pot full in one hand and Miss Emily's cup in the other. We sat drinking coffee for a while, but said nothing of any importance. Finally Miss Emily seemed to make up her mind.

"Hank, Tates did the job and I'm going to tell the newspapers about her confession," she said firmly.

Hank put down his cup and faced her. "You know better than that," he said. "Who are you trying to protect?"

"What's the difference? Tates hasn't any family to care. And she'd be willing to have the world think she killed Bertram's wife because she was jealous, and she killed Willing to get rid of him—the discarded lover, the papers would say—and then took her own life because she knew that the police were about to make her pay for her crimes."

"You've made a nice story, Miss Emily. Too bad we can't do it. People can't be allowed to go around killing, you know. You said yourself that you and your brother would be the next."

"I'm willing to take the chance. If we were to make the murderer feel safe, then there wouldn't be any other killings. I know that."

"You—may—be—right. It's worth trying, at any rate. All right, Miss Emily. There's a reporter in the cut-room, waiting for me. Go and talk to him. Give him that version and see what happens. But remember, Miss Emily, if anything happens to anybody else, it will probably be either you or your brother Bertram. Are you willing to take the risk for Bertram as well as for yourself?"

She was halfway to the door before she nodded in answer. As we settled down again, Hank said:

"Is Miss Emily very fond of Gaines?"

I remembered her enthusiasm about advertising and the way she treated Gaines like a combination pet and office boy. "He's worked here for years," I told Hank. "Nobody could tell how she feels about him, by the way she acts."

"About Marcia?" Hank's voice sounded desperate.

"Miss Emily likes her mildly, I think. That's all, so far as I can tell."

"Bertram?"

"She loves him sometimes and she'd wipe up the floor with him other times. But he isn't the murderer. He couldn't be. You forget the two attempts at murdering him," I reminded.

"Jake?" Hank looked across the room at Jake's watchful face.

"But somebody tried to poison Jake," I reminded him.

"You forget," Hank said. "Tates did that by accident. There is no reason on earth why that accident should have prevented Jake from doing every one of the murders. He hadn't an alibi, not for any of them."

"Neither had I. Neither had anybody else. You never saw a bunch with fewer alibis."

"Jake's a disagreeable cuss and I hate like hell to leave him out of the murderer list," said Hank. "But he isn't a likely bet, really. There's a much better bet, much closer to hand, Nita. I'm surprised you haven't seen it. Maybe you have."

I knew what was coming, and I sat tight. Very gently Hank said:

"Maybe Miss Emily is the murderer. What about that?"

EIGHTEEN

To me, all indications seemed to point to Miss Emily's
guilt. But I wasn't going to admit it, even to Hank. After
all, who was he? Just a policeman in plain clothes. Just a
man I'd met yesterday.

What difference did it make that I'd made a fool of
myself by falling for him as soon as I saw him? Even the
newspapers saw that was funny.

He was probably just being clubby with me for the
duration of the case. Hadn't I heard, often enough, of
detectives or policemen who played up to unsuspecting
maid-servants and traded kisses for information?

I didn't really believe that, even when I was thinking
it. But I just kept grabbing at reasons for not agreeing to
what Hank was saying about Miss Emily.

"She knew Mary Smith," Hank said first. "She knew
more about her than any of the rest. She knew Mary had
married Gaines first and led him a hell of a life, playing
around with Bertram while she was still married to Gaines.

"Then, after Mary was divorced from Gaines and tack-
led Bertram with the blackmail racket, Miss Emily knew
about that, too. Then Mary married Bertram and left him.
She heard about the jewels and came here to try to get
them. She managed to stay in the store over-night. Twice.

Each time she was interrupted before she could get the jewels."

"How can you be so sure, Hank?"

He didn't pay any attention to me. "Gaines and Marcia talked to Mary that morning, with Agnes in the next room, listening. But there was another door, leading into another room. Somebody else might have been in that room. Somebody else might have slipped into the room behind Mary's back, without being seen by Agnes in the next room, and Gaines on the way out. Why not Miss Emily?"

"Impossible," I said weakly, knowing how lightly Miss Emily walked, how easily she might have slipped in and slipped out again, without any noise except the muffled shriek that Gaines had thought was part of Mary's ordinary tantrums. True, Agnes hadn't mentioned the shriek. But maybe she had heard it anyhow. Agnes didn't always tell everything. I'd learned that by this time, and so had Hank.

Hank shook his head. "Miss Emily is little, but she's strong and wiry. Mary was a fragile little thing. Emily could have slipped up behind her, with one hand over her mouth and the other hand free to grab the sharpened scissors and use them."

I shuddered. "Not Miss Emily. She couldn't. How could she know how?"

Hank said thoughtfully. "I'd bet on Miss Emily to do anything she wanted to do. I sometimes think she knows everything. At least she gives that impression. She could have killed Mary."

"But the others. How—"

He interrupted me. "Maybe Willing came in time to see the tail end of all this. Maybe Miss Emily had to kill him. Maybe Bertram saw something and she tried to kill him too."

"Not Bertram. Not her own brother. If you could hear the way she has talked about him, you wouldn't say so."

"She hated to hurt him, Nita. That's why she made such feeble attempts to kill him. She needed to kill him to save herself. Yet she loved him, in her way, and so she pulled her punches accordingly. I can understand how that happened."

"I don't believe it, Hank."

By this time I didn't. Because I wanted Miss Emily to be innocent, I believed she was innocent and closed my eyes to the appearance of guilt.

"She could easily get the weapons in the sporting goods department, couldn't she?"

Hank took another cigarette. Around us the noise and clatter of the lunch-room roared, but I didn't pay any attention to it and neither did Hank. My plate was a congealed mess of tomato and spaghetti and thin canned corn, and it made me slightly nauseated to look at it. My coffee was cold in its cup, but I felt a little dizzy, so I took a sip of it anyhow.

I nodded in answer to Hank's question. That much I could acknowledge, because I couldn't deny it. Nobody could have taken the knives and guns more easily than Miss Emily.

"Did she know the scissors had been sharpened?"

I nodded, reluctantly. She had been in the office when they were brought back. Hank could check that, so there wasn't any sense in denying it.

"Mary made some sort of curtain speech about using the scissors to kill Gaines, didn't she?" Hank went on.

I couldn't deny that either.

"If Miss Emily was at the other door at that time and heard her, it may have put the idea into her head."

"You're building up a swell case, Hank, but it's all based on the idea that Miss Emily needed Mary out of the way. Why did she? She didn't know Bertram and Mary were married. She thought Mary had been paid off with the cash for the letters. She knew it was Gaines whom Mary came to see. If she thought Mary was after the jewels all she had to do was to call the police."

"And let Mary spill the stuff about the love affair with Bertram?" Hank suggested, looking at Jake, who was getting up to leave.

"Why not?" I asked staunchly. "After all, what did that have to do with Miss Emily? Mr. Bertram didn't have any dignified position to uphold even if he thought he did. He was a bachelor, so far as Miss Emily knew. Miss Emily wouldn't murder people with such slim reasons as the ones you're giving."

Hank grabbed my elbow and turned me around to face him. "Listen, kid, how do you know what's a slim reason and what's a fat one for a murderer? I knew a man once who killed his wife because she bobbed her hair when he didn't want her to."

I didn't want to look at him. I hated him. But I had a little sneaking feeling that he was right and that Miss Emily was the only one around the store who could have done a job as carefully as the one done by the murderer.

Such perfection in timing wasn't careless. It might have been an accident the first time. It might have been pure chance that she—or whoever it was—had found the one time and place when the murderer would not be seen by the man going out and the woman who had just gone into the next room, as well as the victim herself. That might have been luck or deftness in timing.

But the business of Bertram and Tates was not luck. It was sheer genius. The murderer had to pick the one minute when Bertram had his eyes closed after Tates stabbed him; had to hit both Bertram and Tates over the head with something. To stun them. Tates, first, probably, so she wouldn't scream. Then Bertram, while he had his eyes closed.

Hank must have known what I was thinking. He said: "Miss Emily's got brains enough. Efficiency, too. This needs an efficient person. To pick the time when Tates' attention is on Bertram, and Bertram's eyes are closed. Miss Emily might have been hiding behind that counter where the corset case was overturned."

I tried not to agree with him, yet it did sound logical.

"She was surprisingly deft at it," Hank was saying. "If she did it at all."

"She's wonderful." My voice was full of the pride I felt for the efficient way Miss Emily always did things.

"You are pretty crazy about her, aren't you, kid?" Hank's voice was gentle.

I nodded. The lump in my throat wouldn't let me talk. I pushed the cold coffee away from me with a gesture so swift that the coffee didn't slop over into the saucer.

"She wanted to blame it on Tates," Hank continued. "She said Tates didn't have any people and there wasn't anybody to mind. I wish I could do it, kid. She's a swell old girl. Even if she did a dozen murders she's that. And a wrought-iron backbone, too, the kind you don't see often nowadays."

"Let Tates take the blame. After all, she confessed." I didn't know my own voice. It sounded harsh. Old.

But Hank shook his head. "There's such a thing as ethics, kid," he said. "I'm sorry. No can do."

"She didn't do it. She couldn't. I'd sooner blame anybody. Gaines—maybe he was the blackmailer. Maybe he killed them. How do you know anybody came in the other door? How do you know Gaines told the truth? Maybe he's been bulldozing Marcia, too. He didn't tell her he'd been married before."

"Clancy was watching Gaines during Tates' murder. Gaines was under observation when Bertram was shot. And I found out an hour ago that one of the policemen in the store was at the foot of the stairs while he was waiting for Marcia to change her dress. That was when Willing was killed. He didn't move from the step all that time. He might have killed Mary, but none of the others. And whoever did one did the rest. Because the reason for the other killings was that somebody saw too much."

I felt desperate. "Why not Bertram?" I exclaimed. "He was Mary's husband. He hated her because she deserted him. He didn't want her to go back to Gaines, so he killed her."

"And shot himself? And killed Willing? And stabbed himself? And hit himself on the head? And hit Tates on the head? And stabbed her?"

He made it all sound so impossible, but I couldn't let him go on suspecting Miss Emily. Yet there was a murderer, and every clue directed me toward her too.

"Jake? Why not Jake?"

But Hank shook his head. "He didn't know Mary. He'd never seen her before the day she came to the office."

"Then—Rebecca Allen." I felt as if I were throwing all my friends to the lions. But Miss Emily had been so wonderful to me.

"She had more cause than the rest. Her diary. The robbery. Maybe she loved Bertram and wanted to get rid of his wife so she could marry him. Although she liked Willing, too, in a way."

"'Maybe Tates and Rebecca liked both of the men, in a platonic way. Maybe nobody was in love with anybody." Desperately I tried to collect the remnants of my loyalty.

"They weren't unlike, Willing and Bertram. Maybe they liked Willing, both of the women, because they had a chance with him and not with Bertram. I've known cases like that."

By this time the lunch-room was practically empty. Everybody had rushed back to work. I knew everybody in the store was on a twenty-minute lunch schedule and I reproached myself for taking so much extra time. But, after all, tomorrow's ad and the next day's were out of my hands.

Hank said quietly: "We found all the jewels. Miss Emily had them taken down to the bank. They were all hidden in the jewelry department except one pin that somebody was buying from the 67c table. It's worth about a thousand, I think. They gave the customer a $4.95 one in exchange and she thinks we're all crazy."

"It didn't take long," I said. Maybe I was getting suspicious.

Hank wasn't, just now. "The stuff was all in the department and Miss Emily knew every piece by heart. It hadn't been there for many minutes. Nobody had a chance to sell any of it."

"Just as well."

I stood and collected things. Back to the old grind. But Hank caught at my arm. "Look here, kid," he said, "we aren't the way we were yesterday. What's wrong with us? We aren't going to let this business about Miss Emily come between us. Aren't you going to be my girl? I thought we had that settled yesterday."

Resentfully I said: "You'll find you a new girl on the next case, if that's all you want. There ought to be a nice line of telephone numbers wherever you go. That's part of your job, isn't it?"

I flounced away and was out in the hall before he caught up with me. He didn't say anything personal. Just kept talking about the sale and the way people were buying and the way Miss Emily's ad seemed to be getting business even if it wasn't the kind the Better Business Bureau cared much about.

But after he stabbed at the elevator button with a long forefinger, he said, without looking at me: "This job will be over today. Tonight's Saturday. Tomorrow's Sunday. The next day's Monday."

"I know the calendar, too."

"Brat! I'm asking you for dates. I mean I want to go places with you or sit at home with you and a good book and a pet dog or something. Give a fellow a break, won't you, kid?"

I cheered up immediately. "Maybe I will and maybe I won't," I said, popping into the elevator as soon as the door was open.

He followed me and said loudly, so everybody heard: "I'll be wining you and dining you tonight, Nita. It's pay-day for cops. I'll spend all of $3.99 on you and have enough left to buy lunch for the rest of the week."

I felt suddenly so peaceful that even the prospect of digging my way through the crowd on the first floor didn't get me.

I was still feeling kind of radiant when I met Gaines on the first floor and he motioned toward a quiet corner near the back door where the trucks loaded.

"Nita," he said, "can you find your friend Hank Bemis and get him up on the advertising floor right away? I've got something to tell you that I think is vital. I think I know who is responsible for the murders."

Before I could ask any questions he was fighting his way through the crowd again and I set out in search of Hank.

So Gaines had found the murderer.

Was it or wasn't it—Miss Emily?

NINETEEN

It was half an hour before I found Hank and got him up to the advertising department where Gaines told us to meet him. And by that time we were too late.

Nobody had heard the shot.

Gaines looked more peaceful at that moment than he had looked at any time in the past couple of days.

He was lying on the couch, with a bullet through his heart, and he looked as if he had discovered many things in the last half hour. He hadn't been dead very long when we came.

There wasn't much blood outside. At least we couldn't see much from where we stood in the door of the cut-room looking toward the couch where Mary Paul had slept on those two nights.

Hank groaned a little as he went to Gaines and touched him, gently, without moving him.

"Why wasn't I here, Nita? This is too much."

"Poor Marcia." That was all I could say. "Poor Marcia."

Marcia came then, just behind us. She pushed us aside and went to the couch and stood looking down on him, without crying.

Then, blindly, she fumbled for a chair and sat down rather suddenly. I went to her and she held tight to my hand. I couldn't say anything.

"This is better," she said. "I could never have made him happy. He wasn't meant to be happy."

"Who did it, Marcia?" Hank's voice was gentle.

Marcia shook her head. "He knew who the murderer was. He remembered hearing something, just as he left the room. And then he knew. Suddenly. He wouldn't tell me. He said it would be dangerous for me to know. He wanted to tell the police first. But he told me one thing, Hank. He said: 'I'm the last one who is any danger to the murderer. I'll be the last. Nobody else is dangerous.'"

"Do you know what he meant?"

Marcia shook her head. "I don't know. I don't know anything. I want to go home to my mother, Hank. She needs me and I don't know anything. I tried to make Fritz happy and I couldn't. Mary followed him into his life with me. She spoiled marriage for him. Nothing would have been right."

"Mary Smith?"

"Mary Gaines," said Marcia bravely. "I think he loved her all the time, even when he hated her. I didn't want to think so, but I believe it's true. I saw him looking at her that first day. When she came up into the ad office when I was there. Later when she found us, and put on the act, you could see that what she said made a difference to him. She was in his blood, I think. It's too late to do anything about that. It was even too late, I think, before he died."

She was looking at Gaines now, and Hank stepped in front of her to shut off her view.

"Could you bear to tell me, Marcia," said Hank in a gentle voice, "if Gaines had anything to do with black-mailing Bertram?"

Marcia nodded. Her voice was steady, but she held tightly to the arms of her chair and her eyelashes fluttered a little as if she were fighting off faintness. The rouge stood out on her cheeks in odd triangular patches. Her face was dead white now instead of its usual creamy rosiness. Her hair had never looked so black and shining.

"I'm afraid now that he did," she said. "I saw a false beard and mustache the other day in his desk. And the same day I came on him looking at some papers. His two marriage certificates. The one for his marriage with her. With Mary. And the one that is ours."

In a flash of memory I, too, remembered two official-looking papers at which Gaines had been staring one day when I went into his office. I said something about them.

Gently Hank asked as many more questions as Marcia seemed to be able to stand and then he beckoned Clancy and gave him directions about sending Marcia home and getting the routine started for this latest murder. It was the last murder, of course, but we didn't know it then.

I'll never be able quite to shake off the horror of the sight of Marcia's face as, she came back to look at her Fritz again. She just looked down at his sightless eyes. Without tears. Without hysterics.

It was as if she were saying goodbye to a hope that had been her expectation. She didn't even kiss his dead cheek. But she stumbled a little as Clancy helped her out of the door.

This time Hank stuck close to business.

It was impossible to get alibis this time. Or any other time. You never saw a bunch with fewer alibis. When the first murders took place there had been so few people scattered over such a large expanse of store that nobody could swear that anybody else was present. That was yesterday. Today it was worse, because the store was so crowded.

The gun was on the floor, wiped clean, of course. It was just like the one with which Bertram had been shot. Gaines must have gone right upstairs after talking to me, and the killer must have been waiting for him.

If I had only been quicker. The murderer had the crowded store in his favor. It was so hard to find Hank. I had had the telephone girl sounding the store calls all over, hunting for him, and I'd finally come on him in the sporting goods department, checking over the perpetual inventory system to see if all of the knives and guns were now accounted for.

The afternoon was almost over before Hank found me at my desk, finishing up an ad for next week.

His face looked more worn than ever and he was lighting his last cigarette, as usual. He slumped into the chair next to my desk and put his feet up on an open drawer.

"Well, Tates is out of the running," he said. "Miss Emily had her money on Tates."

"Don't joke about it, Hank. It isn't funny. It's terrible."

"Listen, kid, it's my business to get this bird and head him toward the electric chair. That's my job. If you think I'm joking, you don't know me. Well, what've we got? Gaines is dead. Willing is dead. Good prospects, both of 'em, but they're dead. Tates is dead and she didn't do the other jobs. We know that."

"Marcia didn't do it," I was quick to say.

"No. She couldn't have killed Gaines. And whoever killed him did it to silence him about what he knew of the other murders. Marcia is clear."

"That doesn't leave us many."

"Let's make a list. Leave out Charlie, the office boy. Leave out Lane, the store detective. I had him out of the place on errands when a couple of the murders took place, and whoever did one, did all. Leave out Jake. I checked him."

"You said yesterday that most of the sales-people and buyers and stock-girls had alibis. That leaves us only a few."

"You are on the list, Nita?" He didn't even grin.

I took a fresh sheet of paper and put it into my typewriter and put a big "1" at the top of the page. "Now for the whole list of suspects," I said. "What do we know, and what don't we know?"

1. *Rebecca Allen.* My letters were brave and big at the top of the paper and I tried not to think of Miss Rebecca with her gallantry and her pert, snappy remarks and her witty comments. I liked her. And here she was. Down on my list like the rest of them.

"She hated Mary Paul." Hank was thoughtful. I wondered if he was seeing in his mind's eye, as I was, the crumpled figure of Mary Paul, dead because somebody had hated her too much to let her go on living. "Mary had stolen things from Rebecca," Hank dictated, and I wrote down what he said. "She had stolen her diary. Her clothes. She had even stolen her man. Because probably Rebecca is fond of Bertram. He looks like the kind of man a strong-minded woman would adore and protect."

I didn't see how, and I said so. "Besides," I asked, "how could Rebecca have killed Miss Tates? Why, they'd been good friends for years. Both of them had been fond of Willing. Both of them had adored Bertram. You can take it for granted that two women who always like the same men will be fond of each other if they don't let jealousy spoil their friendship."

"And how do you know it didn't?" Hank asked. "Rebecca could have shot at Bertram and knifed Willing because they knew too much about the first murder. Maybe she thought Willing had seen the first murder and had told Tates and Tates was going to tell Bertram."

"Jake comes next, I guess."

But Hank didn't think so. There wasn't any real reason to include Jake among the suspects, and we knew by then that Miss Tates' effort to murder Mary Paul had been the cause of the apparent attack on Jake.

"Shall I put down Ken and Agnes?" I hesitated, after writing "2."

"No," Hank said. "In spite of the appearances I don't think that either of them did the murders. Agnes is a genius in her way. The picture she made of Mary Paul makes you understand why Mary should have been the victim of murder. Yet Agnes could take it out in drawing. I mean that she could get a certain satisfaction out of picturing people as victims and didn't have to victimize them herself. That, Nita, is what is known as psychology. You ought to read a book sometime. I did once."

"That gives us only three," I said, not understanding what he was talking about. "Miss Emily and Mr. Bertram. Miss Rebecca I've put down already."

I put down Miss Emily's name after the "2" and waited.

"Miss Emily could have killed Mary," he began, "to save her family honor or to rescue the jewels. She might have killed the rest of them because they knew too much about the murders. She may have pulled her punches with Bertram because he was her brother and she found she didn't hate him as much as she thought she did."

I didn't say anything, but I fought against the hysteria that tried to claim me. How could he talk that way, as if Miss Emily had done these murders? Didn't he know—? But of course he didn't.

I rushed on toward the third numeral, putting down a neat "3" on the page.

I saw that Hank had an envelope in his hand and that he was studying a wisp of a moist white handkerchief that curled damply out of the flap. "Know who it belongs to?" he asked. Carelessly. As if it didn't make any difference. I didn't touch it. I couldn't. But it looked like any other linen handkerchief to me. One of our store specials that everybody in the house bought at the August Linen Sales.

"Man's?" I asked briefly.

He nodded. "No initial or monogram. A man's handkerchief. But that doesn't necessarily mean that a man used it. You see, somebody has been crying. When I picked this up, it was full of tears. But there was a touch of blood here and there. I think I could convict on one little corner of a thumb-print if the linen hasn't blurred it too much. Linen absorbs moisture funny ways. Tears. And blood."

I shuddered. "Then the case is practically closed? You know who did it? The finger-prints have been taken?"

He nodded. "It may be enough, but it probably isn't. You see the finger-print isn't complete. There was a fold in the handkerchief. And even a bloody finger-print won't convince some juries."

I took up the paper and started to tear it across. "Then why all the nonsense?" I protested. "If you know—"

"Go on writing," he ordered. "Mr. Bertram—he's still a possibility, you know. Maybe he killed his wife when he found that she didn't really love him. Maybe he killed the others so they wouldn't expose him."

"But what about the attacks on him. You're forgetting those."

"Yes. Two attacks. One might have been faked. Two—I don't know. Listen, Nita, this takes a clever murderer. All three of these people are clever. Miss Rebecca and Miss Emily are smart girls, both of them. And look at the smart way Bertram grabbed the spotlight when it came near him."

I had an idea. "Could it have been two of them in cahoots? Rebecca and Emily? Or Rebecca and Bertram? Or Emily and Bertram? That would account for the attempts at Bertram. Maybe he and Rebecca are together in all this and she thought he was going to confess, so she tried to kill him."

Anything but Miss Emily. Anybody but Miss Emily.

And all the time I tried to think of desperate suggestions to draw Hank's mind away from Miss Emily, I kept thinking of her myself. I knew that Miss Emily always used the same kind of big linen handkerchiefs that Mr.

Bertram and the rest of the men in the store used. And she hadn't seemed at all surprised when she went into the murder office.

And we only had her own word for the attempt on her. There were no witnesses, and she hadn't been hurt.

She had hated Mary Paul enough to kill her. I had known that for hours, chiefly from the look in her eyes when Hank was questioning her. She could have killed the rest of them if she felt it necessary to save the situation. She could do anything, Miss Emily could. I didn't doubt it.

TWENTY

By this time we were used to answering questions. We knew most of the answers. And since we were quite certain that no customers had gone above the sixth floor we didn't have to let anybody know what had happened except the people who had been in the store the day before. That meant us.

The expression on Miss Emily's face frightened me. She looked older and more haggard than I had ever seen her look. That smooth, marcelled look she had always had was gone. Nothing had come to take its place except a lack of serenity.

I kept as close to her as I could, trying to be reassuring. She didn't do the murders, I tried to tell myself. Yet if she didn't, why was the frightened look in her eyes? Unless she was sure that she or her brother would be killed next. She wouldn't be afraid for herself, but she might for Bertram.

And when I realized that, I began to look around for Rebecca Allen. She was the kindly, angular old maid with her habit of mothering everybody in sight. She was like Marcia had been with her Fritz, only she seemed to be that way with everybody.

A woman like that couldn't have done the murders. It was so utterly foreign to the nature she had shown during the whole of my acquaintance with her.

Yet who else was there, if it wasn't Miss Emily and wasn't Bertram? The rest of them were practically cleared.

I felt horror as I looked at the three of them. Each so impossible as a murderer. Yet one of them had undoubtedly committed four murders besides the abortive attempts at the other murders.

And it was like that, when Hank gathered us all in the little directors' room off the auditorium. The crowded store seemed as distant as Mars.

There were so pitifully few of us left now. Gaines and Marcia were gone. Gaines would never return any more. We knew, by now, the part he had played in the brief shallow drama of Mary Smith's life. He had married the young actress and been baffled by her lack of response to his love and her desire to get him back after their divorce. As Marcia had said, Mary was in his blood. She was part of his dream of marriage, and she would have made his later marriage with Marcia unhappy. At least Marcia would have his child now, and I knew Miss Emily would always see that Marcia was taken care of. Unless—but I wouldn't even consider that Miss Emily might herself be the person who had removed Gaines as well as the other victims.

Poor Miss Tates, with her shining dark satin dresses with their crisp white collars and cuffs. She was gone, too. And Willing who had secretly loved her.

Hank said: "Clancy, you know about these statements. Now, Mr. Bertram, I want to hear your story."

"I was in my office," said Bertram with dignity, "crying." Everybody looked up at him, and he added, "After all, Miss Tates and I had been friends for years. We were fond of each other. Her death was a terrible shock to me. And my wife—nobody seems to realize what it means to me to have lost my wife of less than a week. Nobody understands quite what a shock this trouble has been to me."

Involuntarily I kept wondering how sincere he was about his tears and his sorrows. He looked rather like a plumper, more carefully tailored version of the carpenter in my volume of *Through the Looking Glass* and I kept expecting his tears to be like those of the gentleman who had eaten the friendly oysters.

It was then that everybody began to look at him so queerly. And I thought of the handkerchief. Miss Emily was sitting beside him on one side, Hank on the other. Miss Rebecca was sitting on the edge of her chair, as usual; Agnes and Lang were in a corner together. Jake was watching Hank with evident interest. I had gotten as close to Miss Emily as I could without actually sitting in her lap.

Nobody else was in the room except Clancy with his notebook and a couple of uniformed policemen behind Hank.

Hank said: "I think we understand exactly why you were crying, Mr. Bertram. Because once you had started you had to go on and on."

Miss Emily said, brusquely: "Tears are like that. Once you start, you can't manage to stop."

"I didn't mean tears," Hank said quietly. "I meant murder."

Bertram straightened up in his chair and lifted his chin high above his collar. "I don't understand you, sir. Are you intimating that I—I, Bertram Paul—am a murderer?"

Miss Emily moaned a little under her breath. As if she felt a sudden pain. Hank said quietly:

"I know that you are a murderer. There is no question to my mind. I have the evidence."

Mr. Bertram said, still pompously: "Your silly evidence can have no reference to me. When policemen don't know their jobs they always try to pick on an important personage in order to satisfy their own egos."

But Hank shook his head. "This last time," he said, "you were careless. You cried too much."

As if against his will, Bertram began to look a little frightened. Hank took from his pocket the envelope and showed it to him. The handkerchief.

Even now the handkerchief was moist. "You are too realistic, Mr. Bertram," Hank said. "You cried real tears."

"Of course I cried real tears. I was grieving for my wife and for a woman who loved me."

"For your wife whom you murdered and for a woman who loved you enough to be willing to pay the penalty herself for all your crimes." Hank's voice was relentless.

"Impossible!" Miss Emily's voice was brusque.

Mr. Bertram said: "Miss Tates confessed to the murder of Willing and Mary. Miss Tates said she had tried to shoot me. She stabbed me. She poisoned Jake."

"That is part of the truth, Mr. Bertram." Hank was still terribly quiet. "Miss Tates poisoned Jake, by accident. She stabbed you—again by accident. She intended to turn the weapon on herself and you tried to seize it. You didn't mean to save her from herself. You just meant to make her death more certain. But she turned on you at the last. She saw what you meant to do, and she tried to protect herself. She saw finally that you weren't worth her sacrifice."

"There was no sacrifice. She turned on me. Why—she meant to kill me. She drew blood. I had to kill her to protect myself."

At Bertram's words, spoken in a defensive, matter-of-fact tone, Hank drew a deep breath, and I saw Emily sway in her chair. I pulled my own chair nearer and put an arm around her. She hid her arrogant head on my shoulder and lay limply in my arms, waiting, listening.

Bertram didn't seem to be aware of anything odd in his speech. Without hurry, Hank said: "You know, of course, that Clancy is taking down your statements, to be signed later, and used in court."

Bertram said: "Yes, but you don't seem to understand how terrible this is for me. The necessity of killing her just broke me all up. It was a terrible thing to have happen just when everything was going so nicely without one single hitch."

"You mean you thought you were safe at last?"

"Yes. Mary was gone. Willing had come in at the wrong time, and of course you see I couldn't let him tell the police what he knew. I told you the truth when I said Tates was responsible for Jake's poisoning. I didn't do that." Bertram's voice oozed a sort of oily self-praise. He wanted to claim credit for not having done quite all the crime in that period.

"How did you do it?"

"Well, Tates was stabbing at me with that knife. I had hidden two of them in a corset box in the alcove in her department. She must have found them. She came at me when I saw what she was doing and tried to stop her."

"Can't you be honest, even now, Bertram?" Miss Emily's voice was cold and muffled. She didn't raise her head from my shoulder.

"Very well, then. She tried to kill herself and I thought it would look better if I tried to get the knife away. I didn't try very hard. Maybe I even managed to get enough in her way so that she would be sure to do a good job on herself while she was at it. She knew then, about Mary. She'd never have let me rest about that. I know women. Well, anyhow, she saw—I mean, she thought I was trying to kill her, so she jabbed at me with the knife and cut me on the cheek and on the forehead. It bled."

"But not so much blood as when you killed Mary," Hank said.

Bertram went on with his story: "I found a heavy small display case in my hand, somehow. I bumped it on Tates' head and she let go of me. Then I killed her, the way I killed Willing. Only he didn't see me. I had come up behind him and the carpet was very thick."

I felt a little sick. Miss Emily straightened up and settled herself back in her chair. She said: "Bertram, what started all this?"

"It wasn't my fault," he said. "These things just happen. I had to get rid of Mary. She made me marry her. She wanted money and you keep my money all tied up in the store. I tried to get the jewels for her, but you wouldn't even let me do that. And later when I tried to get them you found them right away. I don't have a break at all. I never did."

"Why did you have to marry her?" asked Hank. "Hadn't Miss Emily bought back your letters?"

"Yes, but I saw her again the next day. She suggested that we might take a trip to Chicago, and I thought we might as well. We registered at a hotel and she had Gaines there. She had him where she wanted him. Right under her thumb. He didn't have any mind of his own, except when he was with Marcia. That's the way she wanted me. And I showed her who was boss. I killed her. I came right up behind her. Gaines was just leaving. I knew he wouldn't look around, even when she screamed—if she did. That was one of the things she hated about him. He wouldn't pay any attention to her tantrums. She said she had screamed several times once and he hadn't even looked around to see her. He had just gone right out of the door. It made her mad, so she told me. I knew he'd do it again. That was the safest time. While he was right there. He wouldn't turn and see me because he never turned around when he got going. And if she screamed when he was gone somebody might come."

"Did you see Agnes?"

He looked a little blank and Hank turned to Agnes. "Are you sure you didn't see all this?"

She shook her head. She said: "I heard the scream. But I had heard Mary Smith tell Bertram about Gaines not turning around. I thought she was just screaming—as she had always screamed—to attract Gaines' attention."

"Why didn't you tell me?" Hank asked sharply.

She shrugged her shoulders. "I'm telling you now."

Agnes didn't tell everything she knew. She had always been like that. Even now we didn't know how much she knew. Maybe a lawyer could get it out of her on the witness stand, but we never got much more from her than her statement that she had heard footsteps that didn't sound exactly like Gaines' or Mary's; that she thought maybe she had seen the other door close as she went into the room where Mary lay dying, and that she had heard Gaines close the door behind him some time before she came out of the next room into what the papers called "the death office" the next day.

Miss Emily said: "Bertram, Bertram—how could you do this? How could you?" She moaned a little again. And then she straightened up and sat back and planted her hands firmly on the arms of her chair, waiting.

Hank and Clancy were both closer to Bertram now, and I saw that the two policemen in uniform had moved so that they were directly behind him. Just in case, I thought. I had wild ideas of murderers who turned to more murder or self-destruction when everything was lost.

But not Mr. Bertram. He was as pompous and ineffectual as ever. It was hard to believe that he had ever done anything so decisive as murder. He seemed so vacillating, and murder was such a final thing. I couldn't associate him with violence.

Hank's voice was thoughtful, not hard. "Don't you understand what you are saying, Mr. Bertram? Do you fully realize what you have done?"

"Anybody would have done it in my place." Bertram had put on that injured, defensive tone of his. "I just didn't get the breaks, that was all. Anybody else could have gotten away with it, but things just don't happen right for me. I always had luck like that."

"So did Mary. So did Tates. And Willing. And Gaines." Miss Emily seemed to be speaking out of stiff silence.

Bertram looked at her in surprise. "But I've already told you there was nothing else to do. Once Mary got hold of me I couldn't get away from her. You wouldn't want her to handle me like she handled Gaines, would you? Why, he couldn't call his soul his own."

"And now," Miss Emily was inexorable, "he can't call his life his own. At least she left him his life. You didn't."

"But I've explained all that. There was nothing else to do. This was the only way. And there was always the chance that they wouldn't find me out. Especially when I had the brains to fake the attempted murders of myself."

He seemed a little proud of that and when Hank asked how he had done it, he shrugged his shoulders and said:

"If I don't tell, you could never find out. It was simple, really. There's a ventilator right outside the lunch-room. I had the gun hidden there. I shot myself where it wouldn't hurt much. See? My arm is hardly even stiff. I took out a book at the public library a few weeks ago. Just to find out a few things I wanted to know about the best places for wounds like mine. And the other kind."

"Several weeks ago? Then you planned these murders then? Before you even married the woman?" It was a duel now between Emily and her brother.

"A man of brains always realizes that there may be some necessity for drastic action. He never goes unprepared."

"That is a rather expensive piece of preparation for you, Mr. Bertram," Hank said quietly, and it wasn't until later that I had sense enough to know that he had a case of premeditated murder as soon as he discovered the book on medical jurisprudence from which Bertram had made such copious notes.

"We have your fingerprints on the handkerchief, Mr. Bertram." Hank seemed to have forgotten that he had told me they had only part of a fingerprint, which was hardly conclusive evidence.

"You have no right!" For the first time Bertram seemed almost hysterical. "Surely a man has a right to cry if he is unhappy. You don't seem to recognize my position. And is it my fault if a little blood got on my hand, even if I did stand where it couldn't spurt on me?"

His mouth twisted as if in his fastidious distaste for blood he had disregarded his own part in the murders.

"You met Willing outside the advertising office," Hank persisted. "Then Willing heard you tell me that you hadn't been near the place all day. Was that why you killed him? To save yourself?"

"I had to walk very quietly." There was mild pride in Bertram's voice. "Of course he would have told you later that he had seen me. And I had no reason to be there except—for Mary."

I looked incredulously around the room. Everything was so unreal. I heard Bertram telling how he had walked up behind Willing and killed him with one of the hunting knives he had purloined from the sporting goods department weeks before. "In case I needed them for anything," he said.

"For murder?" Hank said.

"For murder," Bertram agreed quietly. "Gaines wasn't happy anyhow. He'd have killed himself. He told me so once. And by dying now instead of later I thought he could save me. I felt sure you'd think he had done everything himself. I intended to write a note on his typewriter and sign it for him, but I didn't get a chance."

"No." I had never heard Hank's voice like that, tense and yet somehow quiet. "You didn't have a chance. Neither did Gaines. You killed him without giving a chance to fight for his life."

"But I'm telling you." Bertram was patient, like a school-teacher explaining something to the dunce of the class: "Gaines didn't want his life. He couldn't help being crazy about Mary—first his wife, then mine. He hated her, but he loved her. He married Marcia, but he wasn't really married to her. Nobody who had ever been married to Mary would ever really be married to any other woman."

I had a swift picture of the girl as I had seen her once. Pathetic, shabby, and yet in some way vital. Even in her cruel adroitness she seemed so real that I could well believe what Bertram said.

"Didn't you think of Marcia? Of anybody but yourself?" It was Miss Emily, trying to make everything come out real, trying to make it believable.

But even she couldn't.

"Marcia would have been unhappy with Gaines anyhow. At least now she'll remember him as he was. She won't have to go on with him mourning through his life over the loss of his first wife—to me." Bertram sounded almost human for a moment. Then I noticed the expression that crossed his face when he saw the handkerchief that Hank still held, and I shuddered away from him.

I lost myself in a daze, thinking of Miss Tates and how little she would have had to live for, with her dream of Mr. Bertram destroyed. She had built her life on her love for him. Willing was just an interlude and everybody in the picture knew it but him. At least he had died thinking that her love was his instead of Bertram's, even if he had met death with a knife in his back.

Hank was asking: "How did you kill Tates? How did you fake the attacks on yourself? Where did you hide the knife and the guns?"

"I've already told you about the attacks on myself. There are ventilators in the corridors. It's easy enough, if you know how, to hide a gun there, with a cord to haul it up by. Or a knife. And you know about Tates. I was sorry it was necessary to do that. Won't you take my word for that?"

He seemed to feel that a mild apology was all that could be expected for a murder.

When Mr. Bertram was safely lodged where he could do no more harm to anybody for the moment, and the case was reasonably complete against him, we were still sitting there in the store which was now almost empty.

Outside the newsboys were calling their extras that probably held more than I myself knew about what had been happening. After all, I knew nothing except what I had seen with my own eyes and what Hank had chosen to tell me.

He didn't tell me until later how he had matched the fingerprints on the blood-stained linen handkerchief within a brief time after the last murder. With the natural blurring it was hard to tell. So he bluffed.

Up until the minute he found the handkerchief he was inclined to put his money on Miss Emily, he told me. "But then," he finished, "I'm always wrong a couple of times before I'm right. Up to the last minute I really don't have an idea. That's why I'm the original pessimist when it comes to police work. There are better detectives walking beats all over town than I'll ever be."

"But you got your man. Clancy says you always get 'em."

"That's blundering into success or something. That's the trouble with me. How can I tell whether a clue is really a clue or only a bunch of torn-up love letters from the wrong guy to the wrong gal at the wrong time? With all the things there are hanging around houses and streets and department stores, how can anybody tell if they're clues or not?"

"They ought to be labelled: 'This is a clue'," I agreed.

He grinned at me, and I discovered with an exciting feeling of pleasant shock that I liked him plenty.

"I want a clue, now," Hank said, "and I don't know where to find it. A clue on whether I've got the inside curve on your time from now on. It would be kind of nice to have somebody around to know when I want a cigarette. You could carry an extra carton in your vanity case."

It was almost two weeks before we got around to talking seriously about ourselves. By that time the District Attorney and Bertram had set up a private fraternal organization. The D. A. says that he never knew a murderer so willing to talk about himself.

The D. A. was even a little sorry when Bertram was all talked out.

About the Author

Minna (Feibleman) Bardon (1900-1974), graduated from Hughes High School in Cincinnati, Ohio, and worked her way through college at the Jewish Settlement community center. She sold her first story when she was 12, and wrote a number of romance, detective, children's, and science fiction tales before writing ten books (at least four of which are mysteries). She married Emanuel Bardon in 1931 and had twin daughters and a son. She worked in advertising, then for *Writer's Digest*. She also wrote book reviews for the Cincinnati *Enquirer*. After her husband died in 1958 she became a social worker, helping women find jobs.

BLOOD-RED
DEATH

MINNA BARDON

Also Available
Coachwhip Publications
CoachwhipBooks.com

Coachwhip
Publications

FEAR
CAME
FIRST

VERA KELSEY

THE OWL
SANG
THREE
TIMES

VERA KELSEY

CoachwhipBooks.com

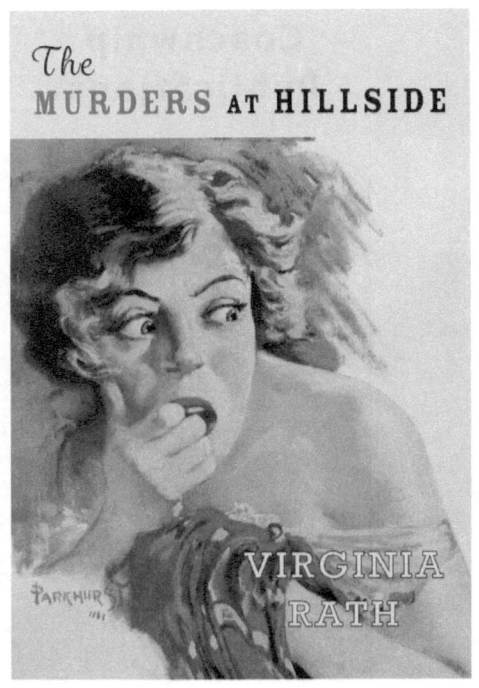

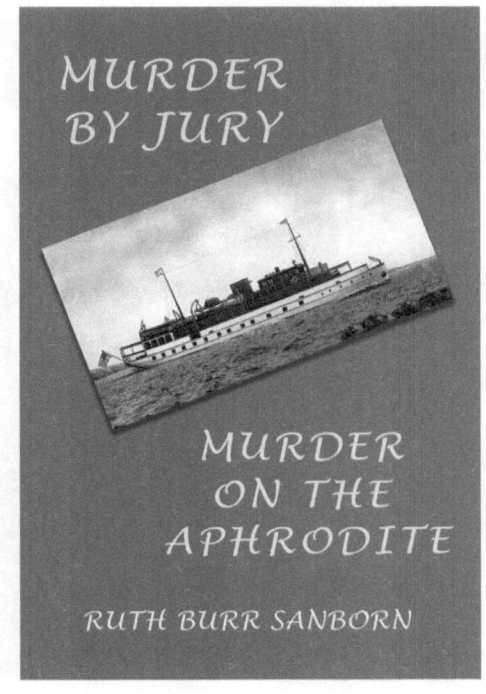

Death Has
Seven Faces

HUGH AUSTIN

Coachwhip
Publications

NARROW
GAUGE TO
MURDER

CAROLYN THOMAS

CoachwhipBooks.com

Coachwhip
Publications

CoachwhipBooks.com

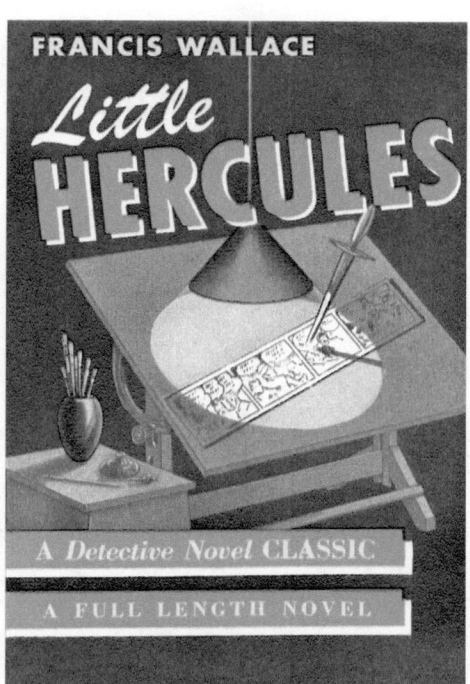

Coachwhip
Publications

CoachwhipBooks.com

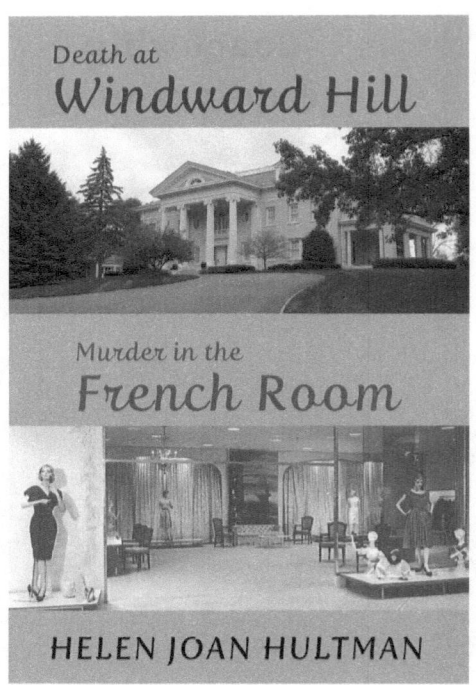

**Coachwhip
Publications**

CoachwhipBooks.com

www.ingramcontent.com/pod-product-compliance
Lightning Source LLC
Chambersburg PA
CBHW021458250626
47154CB00004BA/1377